'Thanks agai[n]... is goodbye.'

He was used to dealing with shocks in A&E. No matter how serious a case might be, it was important to keep a steady face, not to let your emotions show. But this was too much of a shock.

'Really goodbye? Not to see each other again?'

'Well, we might bump into each other occasionally. I gather your A&E department is moving here in six months or so. But otherwise we're back to the situation where you didn't know about the baby. Forget us both.'

'But I do know now! I can't just forget. And...anyway, you've invited me to the christening.' Even to himself it sounded feeble.

'You can come if you want. But you never wanted a baby, did you? And now you don't have to do anything for us. Go back to your old, happy, carefree life. I thought you'd be pleased.'

SPECIAL CARE BABY UNIT

**Special babies, special carers—
lives lived moment to moment . . .
heartbeat to heartbeat**

Dear Reader

My daughter Helen trained as a midwife, but now works mostly in a SCBU. I have seen her feeding a baby so small that she could hold it in one hand. It's work that she loves. It's hard, but so often rewarding.

SCBU work is intensive. The staff—doctors, nurses, ancillary workers—are thrown together in an intimate and often intense working environment. This intimacy often affects their personal lives. It is that very intimacy, and the level of care that I saw being administered to those tiny babies, that influenced me to write this series of stories.

Each of the three stories features a dedicated heroine who discovers that you need more than work to be completely fulfilled.

I hope that you enjoy reading them.

With best wishes,

Gill Sanderson

**Read the next book in this heartrending series
coming soon from Mills & Boon®
Medical Romance™**

A FATHER'S SPECIAL CARE

BY
GILL SANDERSON

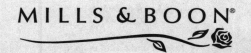

MILLS & BOON®

For Jeanette Ellis—who helped.

*First published in Great Britain 2004
Harlequin Mills & Boon Limited,
Eton House, 18-24 Paradise Road, Richmond, Surrey TW9 1SR*

© Gill Sanderson 2004

ISBN 0 263 83898 6

*Set in Times Roman 10½ on 12 pt.
03-0504-45234*

*Printed and bound in Spain
by Litografía Rosés, S.A., Barcelona*

PROLOGUE

PETRA'S first thought was that it was silly, really. She was being driven into her own hospital by ambulance. She hadn't expected this.

And what had happened was silly. She should have known better. But it had been a fine day, she'd thought she'd get her shopping done before the crowds started. And then, moving a heavy bag from one hand to another, she had had a dizzy spell. Just her luck that she'd been about to walk down a flight of stone stairs.

But, then, she hadn't been too lucky recently.

She had fallen, losing her bag, tumbling like a dropped doll. She had hit her head so there was a lot of blood—scalp wounds bleed heavily. That's why she was vague and confused, she had lost consciousness for a moment. But she was coming to now.

Then she realised there was more. She clutched her distended abdomen, knowing there was something dreadfully wrong inside. And suddenly her life fell apart.

For weeks now the baby had been the most important part of her life. She had felt its first tentative kicks, seen its tiny body when she'd gone for a scan. Her baby. It had taken over her life, all the decisions she made were determined by how they would affect her baby. She wasn't one person but two persons in one. All the time she thought about her—or him. She lay in bed at night holding herself, smiling at the movements deep inside her. This would be a strong baby.

There hadn't been too much love in her life. Now she was amazed at her capacity for feeling. This baby was *her*. When it was born they would love each other with a power that she hadn't known existed.

But now her baby was hurt. She had smashed into railings as she'd fallen. And there was that pain, deep inside. And a dampness between her legs.

'My baby, what's happening to my baby?' she screamed.

The paramedic in the back of the ambulance squeezed her hand. 'Soon have you to hospital love. Then everything will be all right.'

Would it? With a strength she hadn't known she had, she stopped screaming. Panic could only harm her baby.

First she was taken to A and E, now too anxious even to sob. The triage nurse passed her through at once, called for the senior doctor on duty. She was hustled into a cubicle, her clothes cut away and after a thorough examination, particularly of her head, she heard the doctor's sigh of satisfaction. 'Just a cut. No sign of fracture, there's no problem here.'

But they both knew that there was another problem.

'How many weeks gone are you, Petra?' the doctor asked. 'Have there been any problems at all?' He wrapped the sphygmomanometer round her arm.

'I'm thirty-two weeks,' she managed to gasp. 'And

so far everything has been fine. But I feel that something…something's happening there.'

She looked up at the doctor's face and although he tried to keep his expression calm and professional, she knew that there was something seriously wrong. 'What's my BP reading?' she asked.

'Don't you worry about that, just leave it all to us.'

'My blood pressure's up, you're thinking I've got eclampsia!' Now this was serious.

Gently, he stroked her shoulder. 'Just lie there, try not to worry and let us get on with our job. We're sending you straight up to Obs and Gynae, there'll be someone there waiting for you and they'll get everything sorted out.'

She heard a rattle outside. 'There's the trolley,' he said. 'Let's get you moving.'

Of course, she knew most of the team up at Obs and Gynae, she had worked there herself when she'd trained as a midwife. But coming up as a patient, things were different. The consultant still had his usual cheerful smile but there was a detachment in his manner. Now she wasn't just a friend and a colleague—she was a patient. Their relationship was different.

His examination was swift. She watched him as he listened to her baby's heartbeat. 'Thirty-two weeks,' he muttered. 'Well, that shouldn't be too much trouble. Petra, when you fell you ruptured the amniotic sac. The fluid's leaking. And I don't like the way its heartbeat sounds. This baby wants to be born now. But we haven't time for nature to take its course, you need a Caesarean.'

'Is my baby all right?'

'So far as we know, he or she is fine. But we don't
have much time. Now we'll get you prepped, the
forms signed and I'll see you in Theatre.' He smiled
reassuringly. 'Everyone gets good care, you know
that. But these people are your friends, you'll get the
best care there is. Try not to worry.'

How many times had she said that to an anxious
mum? Now she knew just how pointless it was.

'Will I be awake for the operation?'

'I think not. In this case I want a general anaesthetic.'

Another dream gone. She had wanted to watch the
birth of her child. Now the birth would be something
done to her, not something that she did. It didn't matter so long as the baby was all right!

There was a smaller theatre opening off the larger
one. In the larger theatre the consultant performed a
more or less trouble-free Caesarean section. In the
smaller theatre there was a team from SCBU—the
special care baby unit—waiting to examine, to resuscitate if necessary, the newborn child. A thirty-two
week baby should be very viable.

The baby was brought over, laid in the portable
incubator and Chris Fielding, the paediatric consultant, leaned over to examine the infant. This wasn't
an ideal situation. This was Petra Morgan's child, one
of his nurses and one of his friends. It would have
been better if there were staff there who were less
emotionally involved. But there was no alternative
and Chris knew he was the best person for the job.

At first things seemed fine. The baby—a little

girl—was viable, she was taken down to the unit in
the incubator. And in the unit there were more tests.
Blood was taken—almost a tenth of the baby's sup-
ply. The staff needed a haemoglobin count, needed to
know about blood gases, blood glucose, electrolytes.

When the test results came back, the SHO frowned
and looked doubtful. He looked at the baby again.
Yes, she was yellow—but many premature babies
suffered from jaundice. Usually phototherapy got rid
of this—exposure to a bright light in the incubator.
The SHO double-checked the results, then he went to
find the consultant.

Chris examined the baby and looked at the results.
He could feel the atmosphere in the unit changing.
Everyone knew when there was bad news. More people than were necessary seemed to be coming past
this incubator, stopping for a quick word. They were
worried. This child was the daughter of one of their
own.

There was only one conclusion. 'This baby's bilirubin levels are far too high. She isn't going to make
it,' Chris said. 'I suspect the only thing that might
save her life is a complete blood exchange.'

The SHO pointed to a result on the test forms.
'We'll have to use group O for transfusion,' he said.
'The ideal would be her own group. But she's blood
group AB—the rarest of all.'

Chris leafed through the papers in his hand. 'That's
not the mother's group,' he said.

'It must be the father's.'

CHAPTER ONE

IT WAS a day—a night—that shook Dr Dominic Tate's life.

Before that day he had been—well, happy. He was strong, healthy, enjoying life. He knew who he was, what he was doing, where his career was going. At present he was Senior Registrar in the A and E department of Princess Mary Hospital at Calthorpe. But there were going to be changes and he knew that soon he'd be made consultant. Then he'd choose exactly what he wanted to do with his life.

But after that day things were different. He didn't know what he wanted. He wasn't sure what was expected of him. And he was feeling emotions that were new to him. This he certainly didn't like. Dr Dominic Tate disliked doubt and uncertainty in people. And to feel that way himself...

He had had an easy day so far. He had sutured the hand of a farm worker who had cut himself with a scythe and given him a lecture about the necessity of keeping his antitetanus jabs up to date. There had been the usual progression of other small cases and then time for a leisurely coffee. This was a good day!

Later on there was a schoolboy with a fracture of the humerus to X-ray and then set. The usual playground mischief. More seriously there was an old lady brought in by ambulance. She had fractured her hip after tripping while hanging out the washing. The pain was bad enough. But she was desperately worried about her husband.

'Henry's not used to being on his own,' she told Dominic. 'He's getting on and sometimes he gets a bit forgetful.'

'It happens to us all. Are there any neighbours who could keep an eye on him? Or have you got any family nearby?'

Dominic took the phone numbers of a friend and a daughter and promised to let them both know immediately. He also intended to phone Social Services—he had a good relationship with them. They would keep an eye on the old lady's husband.

In the middle of the afternoon things became more serious. A family of holidaymakers came in. There was a large caravan site nearby, with an open-air swimming pool. The Gearing family had been taking advantage of the good weather and had spent far too long sunning themselves by the pool.

Mother, father, eleven-year old Mary, all were suffering from heat exhaustion. Dominic told then to take thing easy, rest in the shade and drink what they could.

But eight-year-old Adam was a different case. He was lethargic, breathing noisily. He felt dizzy, sick, he just wanted to be near his mum. Dominic felt the hot, dry skin, took the lad's temperature. One hundred and three degrees! Unlike the rest of the family, Adam didn't have heat exhaustion—he had heatstroke.

Dominic admitted the boy, arranged for his body

to be sponged and cooled and for his temperature to be taken every ten minutes. 'If it goes up then I want to be told immediately,' he ordered. 'And make sure the rest of the family sit quietly and take plenty of fluids.'

He glanced at his watch. Still plenty of time.

'What a holiday for them,' he muttered to Susie Cash, the ward manager. 'Won't people ever learn that too much sun can be a killer?'

'No, they won't,' Susie said, ''cos they're people, not robots. We're not all perfect like you, Dominic.'

Dominic grinned at her. 'I'm a doctor so I have to be perfect,' he said.

Susie looked at him thoughtfully. 'You're being extra-efficient today,' she said. 'If possible, you're moving faster than ever. Anyone would think that you had something to look forward to. Something planned for the evening?'

Dominic grinned again at his fifty-five-year-old friend. 'I've got a date with the perfect woman,' he said. 'I've even bought a new shirt to impress her with. I'm taking her to dinner at the Fisherman's Rest, and afterwards we'll stroll along the river bank. I'll hold her hand and we'll sit on a bench and watch the sun go down. And after that…who knows?'

'I hope she knows,' Susie said. 'At least, I hope she knows what you're like. Who is this paragon?'

'Melanie Bright. You know, that SHO in Geriatrics.'

Susie frowned. 'I know,' she said. 'Tall and thin and with rather an opinion of herself. But she's going back to South Africa in two months.'

'That,' said Dominic, 'is what makes her the perfect woman.'

Susie looked at him in exasperation. 'Dominic Tate! Don't you think that it's time that you started to—?'

'Dr Tate!' A flustered young nurse came down the corridor 'We've just heard that there's been this RTA. A motorbike accident, driver and pillion passenger both injured, ambulance will arrive in about five minutes. It sounds serious.'

Dominic looked at Susie. 'Let's go and meet it,' he said.

Two black-leather-clad figures were swiftly unloaded from the ambulance and wheeled into the first treatment room. One was moaning, the other completely silent. Dominic walked alongside the trolleys, listening to the paramedic's terse report.

'Apparently going too fast, lost control on a bend. Hit the kerb. Driver was thrown off. Hit a lamppost with his head and shoulder. Passenger hit the road and slid and rolled. We've fitted them both with cervical collars, fastened them to spinal boards. Heartbeat slow and irregular in the driver, fast in the passenger.'

'I'll take the driver,' Dominic said.

His team was waiting and moved into action in the way they had been drilled countless times. The leather suit was cut away. The airway was secured, an SHO introduced IV lines. And Dominic started his preliminary examination.

He suspected quite quickly that this all would be in vain. Breathing was becoming more and more shallow, the pulse fluttery and intermittent. Clear fluid in the ear. X-rays were taken of the skull—massive fractures and evidence of quite deep-seated damage.

The end came quickly, as he knew it would. The body's defences just couldn't cope and the heart stopped. There were the injections, the attempts at defibrillation, everything possible was tried. But it was no use. The young man died.

'How's the passenger?' Dominic asked Molly Grey, his junior registrar.

'He'll survive. Fractured clavicle, flesh abraded from chest and leg, he might need skin grafts. But he'll be OK. I've sent him up to Surgical.'

Molly went on, 'We know any accident is a lottery. That poor driver just ran out of luck. If he'd missed that lamppost he'd have landed in a field of wheat.'

'He made his choice when he drove too fast,' Dominic snarled, and tried to ignore the shocked look on Molly's face. Well, she'd feel that way when she'd attended as many RTAs as he had.

Now there was no end of paperwork. There always was after a death. There were the police, the coroner's office, the hospital organisation that would ultimately get in touch with the next of kin. He learned that the two young men came from Hastings so he wouldn't have to deal with the parents. Not yet anyway.

As usual, when he lost someone, he found it hard to be philosophical. Still, there was nothing he could do now. He had to get on with his own life. And there was an hour before he was due to pick up Melanie.

He walked over to his little hospital flat and found another problem. He'd received an e-mail from a local solicitor, asking for a further report on a farm accident that had occurred a month ago. It was needed urgently as there was a preliminary hearing the very next day.

Usually Dominic tried to keep clear of police cases and claims for damages. He was a doctor, not an insurance agent. A farm worker had been brought in with a crushed chest and he needed support with his claim. A piece of badly stored machinery had fallen across him and the man was lucky not to have been killed instantly. It turned out later that the manager of a big farm had ignored no end of health and safety regulations, the farmyard had been a death trap. Now the manager's insurers were claiming that the farm worker had a pre-existing chest condition and so compensation should be less.

It didn't take long to access his case notes on the computer, and even less time to compose the report he had been asked for. He e-mailed it at once. And then, at last, he was free to enjoy his evening. It was a gorgeous evening; the air was full of the scents of summer. He was going to enjoy himself, this might be an evening to remember.

He laid his new shirt and a lightweight suit out on the bed. Then he went to shower. And when he came out of the shower, only a towel wrapped round him, his doorbell rang. Who could this be? The last thing he needed now was visitors.

Without bothering to pull on his dressing-gown, Dominic opened the door. 'Yes?' he snapped.

Outside was a tall, thin, youngish-looking man in glasses. He looked at Dominic nervously. 'I'm Dr Bradley—Simon Bradley. I'm an SHO at the paediatric unit over at the Wolds Hospital in Denham. Could I have a word with you?'

The Wolds Hospital was the sister hospital to the Princess Mary. In time—in a few months—the Princess Mary Hospital would be closed and the A and E unit amalgamated with that at Denham.

'I've finished work for the day, Dr Bradley. Can't it wait?'

'No, it can't wait.'

Somehow, Dominic wasn't sure how, Dr Bradley had managed to insert himself into the flat, had closed the door behind him. In his quiet way he was determined. This annoyed Dominic.

'Yes, what is it, then?' Dominic wanted to get rid of this young man and he didn't mind showing it.

Simon's words came out in a rush. 'I want you—that is, you're needed—to come to the SCBU to give blood,' he said. 'You're needed right now.'

'Sorry,' Dominic said, not looking sorry at all, 'but I gave blood three weeks ago. A special request, pulled me out of the department to give it. So I'm not due to give more for five months. He went on, 'I'm sure Denham can't be so short of blood that it needs mine.'

Simon swallowed but said nothing and for the first time Dominic felt a little uneasy. There was some expression in this man's eyes that he didn't like. It couldn't be pity!

'Would you like to sit down, Dr Tate? It might be a good idea.'

'It isn't a good idea and I don't want to sit down. I have to go out shortly and I'd like you to tell me what you want with me. And I'm certainly not going over to Denham to give blood. Let them sort out their own mistakes.'

'Mistakes,' Simon said. 'Yes, there have been some mistakes. Do, please, sit down.'

So Dominic sat. Now he was definitely uneasy, he didn't like this. So perhaps he spoke with more venom than was necessary.

'Can we get this over with? And once again, I'm not going to Denham. Why my blood above all others?'

'Well, we only hope that your blood will do. We'll have to check first. There's a premature baby in the special care unit. Her blood group's AB and you're our best hope.'

'I'm your best hope? Why me?' Dominic laughed incredulously.

'Because you're the baby's father.'

There was silence for a moment, and the words seemed to hang in the air between them.

Then Dominic laughed again, in disbelief. 'You're mad. I can assure you that I'm not the father of anyone. I would know, wouldn't I?'

'Apparently not,' Simon said with some distaste. 'Look, d'you remember going to a New Year's Eve party at the Denham Hospital Social Club? You met a girl called Petra.'

Suddenly, Dominic felt there wasn't enough air in the flat. He took a great breath, then another. He rubbed his neck, squeezed his eyes as if to blot out a memory. But the memory was there.

'I remember meeting a girl called Petra,' he said.

It took a vast effort to try to keep his voice calm, and he knew he hadn't succeeded.

'Petra Morgan,' Simon said, 'a nurse in the SCBU. A quiet girl with short dark hair and blue eyes.'

'I remember her,' snarled Dominic. 'What's this about her having a baby?'

'A little girl. She was born this morning. She was prem. Petra had a fall and had to have a Caesarean. The baby was thirty-two weeks gestation and we thought she was doing fine at first. But now we find that she's got jaundice. There's a vast amount of bilirubin in her blood, her liver just can't wash it all away. And if the bilirubin persists in the blood, it'll reach the brain and she'll develop kernicterus. And probably die. She needs blood. The mother's won't do.'

'And she claims I'm the father?'

He could see the anger in Simon's eyes. But all Simon said was, 'Well, if you're not the father, or you are and you don't give blood, then the baby will die. The baby's blood group is AB.'

'That's my group, it's rare. I don't usually give donations, when my blood is needed the transfusion service contacts me directly. Anyway, what is your interest?'

'Well, I'm a doctor involved in the case. And I'm Petra's friend.'

'Just a friend?'

Dominic watched Simon's face grow pale, knew he was trying to hold onto his temper. Eventually he said, 'It might interest you to know, Dr Tate, that so far Petra has refused absolutely to say who the baby's father is. Only when we told her that the best chance of saving her baby's life was blood from the father did she tell me it was you. And she made me promise not to tell anyone.'

All Dominic could do was sit there. Simon must have taken pity on him as he found his way to the kitchen and fetched Dominic a glass of water. Dominic sipped it, his mind a maelstrom.

Not ten minutes before he had been living a happy, hopeful life. Now everything had been turned upside down. He just did not know what to do, think or feel. And he hated it.

Perhaps it could all be a mistake? But he knew this was not likely. Simon's story seemed all too true.

Of course, one thing was absolutely definite. If there was any chance that his blood could save this baby's life, then he had to give it at once. There would be time for thinking, for working out the future, for deciding what he felt, what he had to do—all that could come later.

'Go and get everything set up,' he told Simon, 'I'll get dressed and follow you to…SCBU?'

'I'll have everything set up. We'll need a blood sample just to check, and then take some for the baby. There won't be time for the usual tests against infection, we'll just have to chance that. I'll phone the consultant, he'll be there. You will be there, won't you, Dr Tate?'

'Don't push me too far! I said I'd be there. And I will.'

Simon left. Dominic phoned Melanie, told her that things had come up, he couldn't make dinner. She wasn't very happy about it. Well, too bad. Then he ignored the suit on his bed, pulled on his usual summer outfit of white T-shirt and chinos. Time to go to Denham SCBU.

Simon was waiting for him. 'You understand that your blood will be of best use if you are the father?'

'Well, I suppose I could be the father.' Neither of the two liked that answer, for different reasons. But it was the only honest one.

'We'll take a sample to test first,' Simon said, 'then we'll let you know.'

Dominic nodded. This was the kind of thing he had done so often himself. He was shown into a waiting room.

He didn't have to wait long. Simon came back and said, 'The odds against you being the father are billions to one. You have a daughter, Dr Tate.'

'You'll want to take the blood, then,' Dominic said.

It didn't take long to draw off what was necessary. Prem babies didn't have much blood. When they had finished Dominic said, 'I suppose I'd better go to see Petra.'

'I don't think that's a very good idea. Anyway, she's sedated.'

Dominic didn't like being told what to do by an SHO. But he had to put up with it.

'You're going to transfuse the blood at once?'

'Every minute counts now. Would you like to watch? I gather you haven't seen your child yet. We usually keep parents away for procedures like this, but you are a doctor.'

'I know I am. And, yes, I'd like to watch.'

Your child, your daughter. The words were accurate, he supposed, but every time he heard them he couldn't help feeling a shock. It just didn't seem fair.

The atmosphere in SCBU was radically different from the bustle of A and E. There were none of the swiftly rattling footsteps, none of the urgent calls, none of the atmosphere of controlled panic. Things were calmer here. But there was still the feeling of efficiency, of dedication.

He was introduced to Chris Fielding, the paediatric consultant, who shook his hand in a reserved manner, thanked Dominic for coming and asked, 'You are the child's father?'

'Apparently I am.'

Chris nodded but made no comment. He went on, 'Well, the baby is very ill, I think Dr Bradley has told you. But if we can replace most of the baby's blood with yours, then the bilirubin levels should subside considerably. Anyway, we're grateful to you and we're hopeful. Thanks to you, the baby now has a fighting chance. Do I gather you want to watch the transfusion?'

'Yes, I think I would.'

'Parents are always welcome.'

He was given a gown and mask, taken into a tiny side ward. And there, a tiny pink form in a transparent incubator, dwarfed by the banks of equipment behind her, was his daughter.

His immediate reaction was an ever greater rage. Why had this happened to him? He didn't want a daughter, hadn't asked for a daughter, she was nothing to do with him. But then he realised, like it or not, she was something to do with him. She had half his genes. And if he hadn't wanted a child—well, no one had asked her whether or not she wanted to be born. Dominic found himself feeling a strange kinship with the child. They were both hard done by.

He had witnessed and performed many transfusions, but none into a child as small as this. He stood back and watched. And it gave him an odd feeling to know that the blood being dripped into the child was his own.

First a little blood was taken from the baby by means of a tube introduced into the umbilicus. It was discarded. Then his own blood was introduced. And everyone kept looking at the monitors. Too rapid infusion of the blood could result in shock and cardiac failure. There was a danger of apnoea or brachycardia—the baby could stop breathing or the heartbeat become far too slow.

It was a long and painstaking procedure, taking easily two hours. There were stools for the nurses and two doctors to sit on, but Dominic elected to stand and watch.

Eventually there was a murmur of satisfaction from the medical team. Chris turned and nodded to him. 'We've done all we can now and I'm reasonably hopeful. It's up to Baby Morgan now. If she can pull through the next few hours...well, I'll feel a lot better. You know your blood gave her the best chance she had?'

'Dr Bradley did explain that to me—quite forcibly.'

Chris gave a small smile. 'Simon is dedicated to

his work,' he said. 'Now I'm leaving and there's nothing you can do here. Do you want to leave us a telephone number? So we can let you know how things are going?'

The words seemed to come out without him knowing about them. 'Is it all right if I stay here?'

'Of course. As I said, parents are always welcome. I'll let the nurses know you're staying.' And then he was gone.

Dominic moved over to stare down at the tiny figure, the ludicrously large nappy, the still-yellow skin, the wrinkles on the face. His child? He just couldn't understand.

A nurse who introduced herself as Erica was on duty, and Simon came in and out of the room from time to time to check the monitors. After two hours there was a blip—the oxygen saturation level seemed to go down. Erica came out of her office, looked at the monitors, stared at the baby. 'We get little fluctuations like this,' she said. 'It's not necessarily bad news, it just happens.'

'I know. I'm a doctor.' Then he realised how irritable he had sounded and said, 'I'm sorry. I'm just not…not used…'

Erica put her hand on his shoulder. 'Don't worry,' she said, 'we know how parents feel.'

She was another person to use the word. He was a parent.

The blip was soon over, the oxygen level rose and things seemed to be normal again. In fact, Erica told him, Baby Morgan was doing rather well. She brought Dominic a coffee and said, 'I gather you've got to work tomorrow. Why don't you go home now? I've got your mobile number, if there's any cause for concern I'll let you know.'

Probably that was the right thing to do. But there were other things he had to worry about. 'How's the…the mother?' he asked.

'Petra? She's up in the obs ward, sleeping. Last we heard she was doing as well as could be expected.'

'I'd like to see her.'

'In the middle of the night? I don't think that's a particularly good idea. Why do you want to see her anyway?'

He wasn't used to having to explain himself to anyone, but perhaps this was another thing he'd have to get used to. He said, 'I really don't know. I've seen the baby. Perhaps I ought to see the mother as well.'

Even to himself it sounded a nonsensical remark. But Erica seemed to understand. 'I can phone and say you're coming up for a very quick visit. You'll be let in then. People are careful, you know. Petra has a lot of friends in this hospital.'

'So I gather.' He didn't want to argue.

He was expected at the ward. The nurse let him in with a neutral, rather than a friendly greeting. Perhaps there was an undertone of hostility. He wasn't sure.

'I'll have to stay with you,' the nurse said, 'and it can only be for a minute. She needs her rest, and even when you're asleep people can disturb you.'

'Of course,' he said. 'How is she doing in general?'

'The Caesar was straightforward, no trouble. A shock to the system, of course, but she'll soon be over it. If the baby thrives, so will she. How she's going to cope afterwards as a single mother I just don't know.'

He didn't rise to this, though he felt like it. But he supposed they were entitled to think the worst of him.

He was led to a side room, which Petra had to herself. The nurse switched on a shaded light and he looked down at—at the mother of his child?

She was very pale. She looked incredibly young. Her best feature, her startling blue eyes, were, of course, closed. He folded his arms, stared down at her and wondered why it was that he should have to find out about being a father in this shocking fashion. And he wondered what she thought of him.

'Why the bandage on her head?' he asked.

'Apparently she fell down some steps. Banged her head, shook up the baby so she had to come in for a Caesar.'

'Not a good start for a birth.'

Petra moaned in her sleep, turned over restlessly. The nurse touched his arm. 'You'd better go now,' she said. Then, with a hint of kindness that she hadn't shown up before, she went on, 'You can always come again.'

Could he come again? Did he want to? What purpose would it serve?

It was good to get out into the night air, to feel the dampness and savour the faint smell of salt in the air. In the east there was the faint lightness that suggested dawn would be soon. A new day.

He knew he was more tired than he realised. He had seen too many motor casualties in A and E that resulted from people not knowing just how fatigued they were. He would have to be careful.

He drove back towards Calthorpe. He was on duty early the next day—in fact, today—he had to be there. Be efficient. He needed to sleep to make sure he could give his best. But tired though he was, he knew he wouldn't, couldn't, sleep yet.

He pulled off the road, got out of his car and stared at the dim line of the hills in front of him. Then he glanced at his watch. Only seven hours since Dr Simon Bradley had arrived at his flat and turned his life upside down. It seemed an age. And he knew he had put off thinking about what he had to do, about what he felt. Perhaps it was time now.

He had never been someone to evade his responsibilities. He was now father of a child, he would see that the child was looked after. But there was a bigger problem. What about Petra? He had only known her a few hours—and those few hours weren't very clear. He shook his head. It was no good. Right now he just couldn't think about Petra. Not yet. In time it would be possible. In fact, in time it would be necessary.

He had been in just one longstanding relationship. Only one partner, but she had taught him that with any relationship there was bound to be pain. But...now he was a father. How did he feel about that? In his breast he felt the churning of deep emotions—but what those emotions were he couldn't specify. To his horror he felt his eyes pricking. Him cry? He was tough, an ex-soldier, he could face anything. He hadn't cried since he was nine. He must be tired, that was it. He would forget this situation for a while.

He drove back to the hospital, climbed into bed and was asleep at once.

CHAPTER TWO

PETRA MORGAN awoke with a shock. Where was she? There was a fuzziness in her head, a pain in her abdomen...then she remembered. In a panic she felt for the button that would summon the nurse, pressed it as hard as she could.

The nurse was with her in seconds. 'My baby,' cried Petra, 'where's my baby?'

'She's doing fine. I rang SCBU not five minutes ago. Your baby had a good night and is doing fine. We'll wheel you down to see her later on.'

Then the nurse remembered to be cautious. 'Of course, she's not out of danger yet, but there's a lot more hope than there was last night. Needing the father's blood! That scared everybody.'

'Did he...? The blood... I gather there was a donor?'

'Dr Bradley arranged it. Apparently everything went very well.' The nurse knew that it wasn't her business but she was curious. She went on, 'The...father came in to see you last night. Of course, you were asleep.'

Petra thought about this. 'If he comes again,' she said flatly, 'I don't want to see him. If he phones I don't want him to have any details about how I am, I don't want any messages from him.'

28

'Are you sure? He was very…quiet when he came last night.'

'I'm sure,' said Petra. 'I want nothing to do with him.'

'Your decision. Now, just a few obs and then we'll organise you some breakfast.'

She knew the routine, she'd performed it herself often enough. And after a while she had been fed, helped to wash, her wound inspected and dressed. She had a new nightie—this time one of her own. Her pillow slip was changed. The old one had been damp—through tears. And for a while she was left alone to think.

Her baby. Her little girl. She hadn't even decided on a name yet. After all, she had only been thirty-two weeks pregnant. Yesterday morning had started as normal. She had still been living in the nurses' home, hadn't even thought about where she was going to go to live after the baby was born. She'd better start thinking now. If only she hadn't felt dizzy, fallen down those steps!

She'd felt as happy about the Caesarean as anyone could have in the circumstances. Her baby was premature, but she would be looked after by members of her own team. Her unit would fight like demons to help her baby. She had every confidence.

And then, while she'd been coming to, still in considerable pain, Simon had appeared by her bedside. He was her friend, hadn't he known that she'd wanted to be left to sleep? But Simon had been urging her, demanding that she stay awake. Her baby had needed blood. And the best blood was the father's blood.

Who was the father? She had to tell him—who was the father?

She hadn't wanted to think about the father. She had refused to tell anyone his name. This was her problem, her baby. She would tell no one the father's name.

Even in her half-drugged state she'd been able to tell that Simon had been in torment at having to upset her. But he'd done it. He'd forced himself to say it. 'Petra, if we can't find the father to give blood, then your baby could possibly die.'

So she'd gasped out the name and where the man could be found. 'Dr Dominic Tate. He's in the A and E department at Calthorpe. Ask him...ask him if he remembers the New Year's Eve party.' Then she had wept again, and shortly afterwards had been sedated.

Now, she supposed, she had to plan, to think. She had a baby. And she hadn't even got anywhere to live.

She considered, and there didn't seem to be many options open to her.

She was an orphan, had no relations of any kind. She had no home to go to. For three years she had shared a house with Ken Bannister, her one-time lover. But that had been repossessed and she'd discovered that Ken had taken all the savings from their joint account when she'd finally left him. And then she'd had one—just one—moment of madness and had found she was pregnant.

She turned her head into her already damp pillow and wept again.

But she still had friends. For the morning she had

to stay in bed. She could go to see her baby later in the day. Her friends from the unit brought her flowers and photographs of her baby. They all wanted to see her but didn't want to overtire her. Petra found this comforting.

At lunchtime Simon came in to see her. She was glad to see him. Over the past few months he had been a real friend to her. She'd wondered if he wanted more than friendship. But for the moment Petra was right off love. Still, it was good to see him. And he brought even more flowers.

'How's my baby?'

Simon leaned over, kissed her on the forehead. 'Your baby is holding her own. Yesterday she gave us a scare, but now things are better. Now, how are you?'

'Well, I'll feel far more sympathy for mums in the future. I thought I knew how bad it was, now I know I didn't know the half of it. But I'll survive. Simon, I owe you, don't I? I owe you my baby's life. You made me tell you the name of the father—and then you fetched him.'

Simon blushed. 'It was nothing. I'm sorry if I was a bit rough with you but we just had to know. And now it's all worked out well.'

'Yes. Dr Dominic Tate. How did he...? What did he think? I never wanted to have anything to do with him again. But how did he take the news that he was a father?'

Simon frowned. 'It's hard to tell. He's obviously used to hiding his emotions, he comes across as a hard man. Perhaps he is a hard man. But once I got

the message across he said at once that of course he
would give blood, he couldn't have been more co-
operative. And he asked after you.'

'Did he talk about me? Tell you what happened?'

'Not at all. And I'd be too scared to ask. He phoned
me this morning, he wants to see you as soon as
you're well enough.'

'I don't want to see him. Ever!' It was an instant
answer, she didn't even have to think about it.

Simon seemed uncomfortable, reached across to
stroke her hand. 'I think you ought to see him. In a
hard way he seems to be quite a thoughtful chap. Do
you know, after the transfusion last night, he stood
for three hours watching the baby and didn't move a
muscle?'

Petra frowned. She had seen that stillness, that stare
on the faces of parents before. It was as if they believed that just by looking, hoping, they could help
their child survive. She hadn't thought that Dominic
would be so bothered.

'I still don't want to see him,' she said. 'I've got
nothing to say to him.'

'That is your decision. But you'll have to see him
some time, you'll bump into him. You know they're
closing down the Princess Mary hospital at
Calthorpe? And A and E will be moving here? Well,
Dominic Tate is tipped as the next consultant.'

She thought. Well, if she had to meet him then she
might as well get it over with. 'OK, tell him to come
tonight. I'll see him just for five minutes.'

'Would you like me to be here with you?'

'No, but thanks for the offer. I want...I need to face him on my own. Then it will all be over with.'

'Well, if you change your mind...'

He stayed a bit longer, and after a while she found herself crying again. For no apparent reason.

'Are you all right?' he asked in some alarm. 'Is there anything I can do—anything I can get you?'

'Really, I'm fine,' she sniffed. 'You've seen this in new mums before, it's just hormonal imbalance.'

'Other mums are different,' he said. He left shortly afterwards.

Petra lay back on her pillow and thought about the last twelve months. It had not been the best year of her life.

She and Ken had been getting nowhere. She had been enjoying her work, progressing steadily and hoping in time for promotion. But it had been hard—and when she'd come home there had always been the clothes to wash, the flat to clean and Ken to cook for. Even though he'd mostly been out of work—'looking about' he called it—he'd never seemed to have time to help.

She had begun to wonder if she had made the right choice. Certainly Ken was cheerful and good-looking, always the centre of any party. When he had picked her—a quiet girl with few social skills—she had wondered at her luck. Now she was wondering just how lucky she had been.

And yet another of Ken's ramshackle business ventures had been about to crash. He'd wanted to lease a curio shop near the harbour. They had argued for days about it because he'd wanted her to take out a

large bank loan with her salary as security. She'd
wanted to save for a house of their own. And she'd
known this scheme would go bad, like all the others.

Then Ken had come in one night with a satisfied
smile. 'Things are looking up. I've hired a manager
for the shop—Karen Collis, remember her? With her
behind the counter we'll make a fortune.'

Petra winced. She remembered Karen from
school—she was loud-mouthed, idle and petulant. 'I
thought you were the manager,' she said to Ken.

'Don't worry, Karen will get the punters in.'

So Petra decided to say nothing more. But a fort-
night later she left work early and went into town to
do some shopping. She called at the shop and found
it closed. She had a key. In the back she found Ken
and Karen, in the bed he had ordered as a necessary
expense.

She left the flat that afternoon and moved into the
nurses' home. Only when she called at the bank did
she discover that there was no money in their joint
account. Ken had taken it. She was penniless.

But she had friends and a good job. In time she
would pull through. She knew she was now a tougher,
more independent woman. She had learned.

And now she was here, lying in this bed with the
pain in her abdomen where the incision had been.
Always at the edge of her mind was her baby. How
was she doing down in SCBU? She knew what devoted care the baby would get. She also knew that
care was not enough, sometimes a baby's survival
depended on sheer chance. It helped to think about
other things. How had she got in this state.

She had been in the nurses' home for a few weeks and had been quite enjoying herself. Over Christmas she had volunteered for all the unwanted shifts—she had worked Christmas Eve, Christmas Day and Boxing Day. After all, she'd had nothing better to do. But when she'd tried to volunteer for New Year's Eve, the ward manager, Jane—now married to Chris Fielding—had put her foot down.

'No, you can't work New Year's Eve. Take the time off and go out and enjoy yourself. There's more to life than work, I know that.'

So Petra reluctantly agreed that she would join the large group that was going to the New Year's Eve dance at the hospital social club. The social club was in the hospital grounds. She could slip away after a while.

'And what's more,' said a friend, 'you're not going looking like that. When you're out of uniform you tend to look like little orphan Annie. Show the world that you're fighting back. It's a party, you're to dress up. You can borrow stuff if you want.'

She knew it was painful but good advice. She would fight back. 'All right,' she said.

'And make yourself feel wicked. Forget tights, get some stockings and a suspender belt.'

'Wicked but uncomfortable,' said Petra. But she spent a little money and did as she was told.

A nurse who had trained first as a hairdresser did her hair and showed her how to accentuate her best feature—her eyes. She borrowed a blue dress. And when she was ready to walk across to the club with the rest of them she did indeed feel good. Perhaps this was to be the start of the rest of her life.

It was a good party, a good dance. She knew so many people there that there was always someone to chat to, to dance with. She guessed she was enjoying herself. But at her centre she felt a detachment. She was with the party but not of it.

She tried not to drink too much but at times it was hard. Her first intention had been to wait until New Year struck before she left but now she wondered if she should bother. Tonight, this just wasn't for her.

It was curious how she met Dominic. She was standing near the bar, talking to an old friend she hadn't seen for a few days. When they parted she found herself facing a tall man, desperately trying to balance too many drinks on a tray that was too small. It was a party, people were being friendly. 'I could carry a couple of those for you if you like,' she said.

'That would be marvellous. Otherwise I know there will be more in the tray than in the glasses. Could you take those two tall drinks?'

She followed him to a table where six people were sitting. He carefully gave them a drink each. 'Are you going to join us, Dominic?' a lady asked.

'No. I'm going to dance with this young lady. But have a good evening.'

'You didn't ask me to dance with you,' she pointed out as they moved away from the table, 'and you don't have to. Don't you want to be with your friends?'

'Three of them are friends, people who work for me. But they've all brought partners. They're all in love and better off without my company. I don't want to talk shop or about the cost of new houses and furniture.'

'You're just a cynic,' she told him, 'like me.'

She enjoyed dancing with him. She used to like dancing a lot, and now she sang along to the pop tunes that were being played. It seemed natural that at the end of the dance they should stay on the floor.

She looked at him. He was dressed smartly, in an understated way. A lightweight grey suit, dark red silk tie, the whitest of silk shirts. He could have looked just ordinary but he didn't.

His face was at odds with the simple elegance of his dress. It was harsh, tough. His dark hair was longer than was usual, rather curly. His nose had been broken once, it made his face look craggier than ever. It was the kind of face that, if it scowled at you, would make you want to move away. But when he smiled, things were different. She saw the white teeth, the sensuality of the lips.

'We have to tell each other what we do,' he said. 'People aren't people here, they're jobs. What do you do?'

'I'm a person as well as a job, My name is Petra Morgan. I'm a nurse in SCBU and I love it. What about you?'

'Specialist Registrar in A and E over at Princess Mary,' he said laconically. 'Are you with anyone—a group or anything? I didn't mean to kidnap you.' It was asked casually, as if just to make conversation.

'I came with a big gang of friends from the nurses' home. I wasn't really keen but they were determined that I should have a good time. And now most of them are now wandering off making new friends. Are you with anyone?'

'Same story. Like Cinderella I will fly at midnight but leaving no glass slipper. I'm working tomorrow morning. Would you like a drink?'

'I'd love a glass of red wine.'

'So would I. I'm Dominic, by the way.'

They went to the bar together, he bought two glasses of red wine, and when she turned, holding her full glass, she tripped and inadvertently threw it all over him.

She looked at him, aghast. 'Dominic, I'm so sorry! Your white shirt, it's ruined. And I... Oh, how could I?'

He shrugged, obviously not too bothered. 'It's just a shirt. But it gives me an excuse to leave. I can't stay looking like this. People will think I've come straight from the operating theatre without changing.'

'But it looks new!'

'It is new, Italian silk. Don't worry, I can buy another.'

She realised that he wasn't being polite, he genuinely didn't care. And that made her more determined to do the right thing. 'If you soak it straight away it will be all right,' she said. 'The nurses' home isn't far away. Come to my room and I'll sponge it for you. Then I can iron it dry and you can put it back on and we can come back to the party.'

He looked at her. 'All right,' he said.

That was the beginning. So often since then she had tried to remember what she had really been think-

ing of. Had it been a genuine mistake on her part—
had she really wanted just to clean his shirt? Or had
there been some part of her mind that she'd known
nothing of, that had deceived her? Had she thrown
the wine over his shirt on purpose? Had she…had she
wanted him—if only for the night?

She just didn't know. But he had been very attractive. They'd walked to the nurses' home, now almost
completely deserted. Back in her room she'd told him
to sit down, take off his shirt.

He'd taken off his jacket, tie, unbuttoned his shirt.
He'd had the body of an athlete. She'd seen the pow-
erful muscles, the narrow waist, the wings of dark hair
across his chest. He'd seemed totally unselfconscious
about being half-naked and that had made her easier.

He looked round her room, saw the stacked storage
boxes. 'Moving out?' he asked.

'I've just moved in, there's nowhere to put things.
I was in a relationship and it…fell apart.'

To her surprise she saw a quick flash of pain across
his face. 'They do,' he said.

For a moment they just looked at each other. She
knew that she'd had more to drink than usual—but
not a lot more. Perhaps a single glass more. But she
knew what she was doing. No, that was wrong. She
didn't know what she was doing.

She realised she was still clutching his shirt. 'Sit
here and I'll fetch you a drink,' she said. 'I can borrow some wine from out of the fridge and I'll rinse
this through and put it in the drier.'

'There's no need to go to so much trouble.' But
she fled anyway.

She managed to get most of the red wine out of his shirt. She squeezed it then put it in the drier. After fifteen minutes it would be ready to be ironed. Now they would have a glass of red wine each and talk for a while.

He stood as she entered her room, a tall imposing figure, naked to the waist. 'I've brought you a glass of wine,' she faltered.

'You're very good to me.' He took both glasses of wine from her, set them down on her little table. Then he leaned forward and kissed her, very gently, on the lips. He didn't attempt to hold her, touch her with his hands. She thought this was a signal. Whatever might happen, she could easily escape.

Suddenly, outside there was a great noise. There were yells, the sounding of church bells, the banging of the gun from the yacht club in the harbour. It was midnight. A new year starting. She moved away from him, switched off the light and opened the curtains. Great arcs of light flashed across the sky—a firework display.

She was side by side with him now. He put his arm round her shoulders. She could feel the warmth of his body against her arm and the bare skin touching sent flashes of excitement though her body.

'Are you going to make any New Year's resolutions?' he asked.

'I've done it before and it's never been successful. All I'm going to do now is wait and see what happens.' Was that forward? She didn't intend it to be.

Now there was a bang and great streams of silver stars flared across her window. Petra could see him

by their light, his head and body a pattern of light
and shadow. And he kissed her again. This time it
was different. His arms were round her, gathering her
to him, pressing their bodies together. But still not
too hard. She knew he was holding back, that if she
wanted she could disengage herself, pretend that this
was just a New Year kiss. She was grateful to him
for that. But both of them now knew that this was
more than a holiday kiss. It was a prelude to something more.

She was not going to turn back. All her life she
had been good—at school, in nursing training, to the
ancient aunt who had brought her up. And what had
it got her? A spoiled life with a man who had seen
her as another little convenience. Well, for once she
would act madly, do whatever her body told her to
do and forget being good and practical.

She stepped back from him, reached behind her and
felt for her zip. The buzz as she slid it down seemed
unnaturally loud in the little room. She shook her
shoulders, the expensive dress fell in foam round her
feet. She stepped out of it. Fireworks flared again
through the window and in their light she could see
her own body. The untypically lacy underwear, the
darkness of her suspenders. What would he do now?

His breath hissed as he looked at her. His hands
reached out, she felt the warmth of his hands on her
arms, but he kept her at arm's length.

'Petra, oh, Petra…' His voice was low but urgent.
'This is so wonderful but I must tell you. There is
tonight but there can't be more. I can't offer you more

than that. After tonight we part and... If you wish, I'll go now.'

She stepped forward and kissed him. 'Then let's have tonight,' she said. 'Just tonight, that's all we need.' In her mind she quickly ran over the past month. No, the time was OK. 'Everything will be all right. There's no need to worry about anything.'

He knew what she meant and pulled her to him. His body strained against hers, his lips touched her mouth, at first tenderly but then with a growing insistence that matched her own needs. For a while they stood there, then she pushed him away, feverishly tore off her few remaining underclothes. She saw that he was naked too.

He lifted her, swung her onto the bed. And then...the rest was hard to remember.

She knew she had been taken to places where she had never been before. He was a man who knew that giving was as pleasurable as taking. Neither spoke, but when eventually she'd heard herself calling aloud in ecstasy she'd known that he'd been doing the same. And outside there had been the loudest of bangs, and the sheen of coloured stars on their bodies.

After a while he'd spoken for the first time. 'You are so lovely,' he said. And, contented, she closed her eyes to sleep.

In the afternoon the doctor came, inspected her incision site and said she could go down to see her baby. She found herself in an odd mood—excited and weepy at the same time. So often she had seen this in the mums on the ward. She had sympathised, of course, but now she realised she hadn't had the least idea of what their feelings had been.

Carefully she was eased into a wheelchair—and it hurt! It didn't matter. Gently she was wheeled down to the SCBU.

This was the place she worked, the place she had spent so many weeks of her life. And now it seemed so different. She was taken into a side ward and there, in an incubator, was her baby. Her vision blurred as her eyes filled with tears. Her baby!

She was surrounded by friends, by people she had known a long time. There was the odd gentle kiss, her arms were stroked, there were quickly whispered good wishes.

She was wheeled to the side of the incubator. A nurse opened it, took out the little bundle and put it to her breast. Of course, her milk hadn't come in yet—but soon, soon. She would have to make arrangements.

So often she had seen this scene before, and she thought she had understood. But now she knew she had no conception of the emotions involved. They were stronger than anything she had felt before.

As she sat there she made a vow to herself. This baby would have every opportunity, every chance. She would see to that! She leaned over, and tears dropped onto her baby's woollen cap.

When she felt stronger she wanted to speak to the consultant, and Chris was waiting to speak to her. He came out, kissed her on the cheek and smiled.

'Things are going pretty well,' he said. 'You know yesterday was bad—it could have been really bad.

Thank Simon for arranging that transfusion, I think it saved your baby's life. But now…well, we're optimistic.'

That was good enough for her. She stayed just a while longer and then was told it would be better if she returned to her bed, it would be foolish to overtire herself. She knew this was true.

She was wheeled back to her ward, tired and in pain. But she was happy. She had seen what—who— she was fighting for. And she was determined to fight.

CHAPTER THREE

So Dominic was coming to see her. Petra didn't particularly want to see him but she supposed she had to thank him for providing the blood. She would thank him, he had saved the life of her baby. The thought struck her that her daughter was half his baby, too, and this she didn't like. But she would thank him and then he could get out of their lives.

She'd decided very early in her pregnancy that she was not going to tell him about the baby. Obviously he didn't want a child. He had been fair, he had told her in her room that it was only to be a one-off occasion. She had made her choice then. If she had told him—mistakenly—that things would be all right, that she would not get pregnant, then that was her fault. He was free of all blame.

When she had woken, the morning after they had made love so wonderfully, he had already gone. She remembered he had told her that he had to work the next day. And she remembered lying in bed anyway, a small satisfied smile on her face. It had been so good. Perhaps a nasty part of her had thought how glad she was that she had parted with Ken. It had never been like that with him.

For a week or two she had wondered. He had said that they would not see each other again—but he could change his mind. He could have sent her some flowers, he could have phoned her. But he hadn't. Well, that had been his decision and he had warned her. And so she hid her disappointment even from herself.

And then, after about a month…well, perhaps it had been the result of coming off the Pill. But after a month she'd known she had to worry. She had bought a pregnancy test kit. The test had been positive.

The irony was too much. For a while she'd laughed. Then she'd cried.

It showed consideration, Dominic phoned the ward and asked what time would be best for him to come. Before he arrived Petra got the nurse to help her look presentable, borrowed a lipstick and some make-up, put on a smart bed-jacket. Then she waited. She was determined not to show it—but she was apprehensive. She didn't know what he wanted. She didn't really know what she wanted herself.

It was funny, she could only remember his appearance vaguely. It had been winter, she'd never even seen him in daylight. The social club, her room—all had been dimly lit. She remembered him best illuminated by the stars from the fireworks. And that was some memory.

So she got a shock when he walked in. There was part recognition, part memory. It came back fully how gorgeous he was! And that made her more angry than ever. He had no right to look that way while she was in pain and in trouble.

The night was warm, he was dressed casually in

light chinos and a white T-shirt. She could see the dark hair on his muscular forearms, remembered his naked chest... She had just given birth, just been cut open, her body was sore in places she'd never been sore before. And yet that same body gave an unexpected jolt of excitement when she saw him. Then she looked upwards, saw the inscrutable face. She wondered what he was thinking.

All her other visitors had kissed her. She hoped he would not. She didn't know what emotions it might arouse in her.

He didn't speak at first. Then he said, 'I brought you some flowers. I didn't want you to be the only mum without them. But I see you have plenty.' He laid a sheaf of flowers by her bed.

'I have a lot of friends,' she said. 'But these are lovely, thank you. Are they home-grown?'

The flowers were indeed lovely. There were traditional, old-fashioned roses and she could smell their scent. They were the only flowers she had received that were scented.

'Not my choice,' he said honestly. 'I asked Susie, my ward manager, what to buy. She said she'd bring me some from her husband's allotment.'

'Please, tell her—and him—how much I appreciate them. I like flowers.' She looked at his still impassive face. 'Did you tell her who they were for?'

'I told her they were for the mother of my child.'

'You were not ashamed of saying so?'

'I am the father. It's a fact now. Half the hospital know about it. And I always try to take responsibility for my actions.'

'Is that what the child is? A responsibility?'

'Amongst other things, yes. May I sit down? I don't want to tire you but I think we have a lot to talk about.'

'Please, do sit down.'

He sat by her bed and she found his proximity just a little unnerving. Now he was closer she could smell his citrusy aftershave, and just a touch of a warm male smell that…

I haven't asked how you are,' he said. 'I'm sorry. Are you feeling better?'

She was honest with him. 'I'm suffering but I know I'll improve. Mostly I'm bewildered. Not two days ago I thought I had quite a few weeks to arrange things. Then I fell down the stairs.'

'Yes. I didn't think that night we spent together would have this outcome.'

He looked at her thoughtfully and she guessed what he was wondering. Angrily she said, 'I know what you're thinking. You want to know if I set out to trap you. If I led you on to make me pregnant. Aren't you?'

'The thought did cross my mind,' he said.

'Well, forget it! I didn't tell you I was pregnant. I didn't ever intend to. I told nobody who the father was. Only Simon managed to force it out of me, and that was because…because my baby was dying.' Now the tears were flowing down her face. 'Now I have to thank you for that, your blood saved her life.'

He looked at her, rather surprised. 'It was nothing,' he said. 'I would have done the same for any baby.'

'Did it feel different doing it for a baby you had fathered?'

'Yes,' he said after a while, 'I suppose it did.'

'How interesting. Now I want you to understand this. I only agreed to see you because you saved my baby's life. I don't want to see you again. I want nothing from you. I'm making arrangements for the future and they don't include you. My baby and I have no need of you. You carry on with your life and I'll carry on with mine.'

'But Petra, I ought to—'

'You ought to do nothing! You owe me one thing and that is to leave me alone. I don't need you, I don't want you. Now go!'

She realised she was crying again. He stood, looking at her, irresolute.

'I said go!' she cried.

He walked slowly out of the room.

It was still early evening. Dominic walked through the pleasant hospital grounds and found a bench to sit on in the shade of a giant oak tree. He had to think.

First he had to think like a doctor. He knew what Petra was going through—not only the pain and shock of the operation, the worrying over her child, but also the hormonal whirlwind she must now be suffering. Everything she said would now be governed by feelings, not logic. He had to allow for that. She might change her mind.

But, having though that, why for seven months had she not got in touch with him? How did he feel about that?

He had to admit that a part of him was glad. He enjoyed the untrammelled life he was leading. His work was satisfying. Regularly he took girls out—but he always told them well in advance that he only wanted a fun relationship, told them not to take him seriously. And usually he picked girls who could accept that.

But now things were different. He had a child. Or did he? Petra had made it very clear that his help wasn't wanted. Well, that would have to be checked. If he had responsibilities he was going to honour them. Working in A and E, he had seen too many cases of irresponsible behaviour resulting in pain, injury and death, sometimes to quite innocent bystanders. His job was to treat, not to judge. But he had vowed never to be so irresponsible himself.

Still, he did feel a little hard done by. He hadn't wanted a child. She was bringing a new emotion into his life and he didn't know how to deal with it. But he would have to.

He realised that he hadn't yet thought about Petra. In fact, he had been avoiding doing so. Lying there in the hospital bed, the pain still showing in her face, she had been so different from the sensual creature he had made love to on New Year's Eve. But not too different. The eyes were as blue as ever—even if the expression in them was totally different.

So think about Petra. At the time he had told her that their evening had been a one-off—just a single encounter that had turned into something hauntingly memorable. Afterwards he'd known he could have got in touch with her had he so wanted. In fact, once or twice, he'd reached for the telephone. Then he'd changed his mind.

Why had he changed his mind? She had been good company, a refreshingly witty talker, and their lovemaking had been something he had since dreamed about. Now he realised he had felt something in her—a desperation, a need that she had never voiced but that he'd been able to detect.

Petra had wanted to be loved.

He hadn't wanted to deal with that sort of thing. He'd wanted his love affairs to be casual—pleasure for both, but nothing long term. And Petra had wanted more than that. So he hadn't phoned her.

Feeling rather angry with himself, not happy with his self-examination, Dominic took out his mobile phone and dialled the SCBU. He asked for Simon, who was fortunately in. Abruptly he identified himself, asked how Petra's baby was.

'I'm not sure she wants us to talk to you about her baby,' Simon said.

Dominic was not going to be put off. He snarled, 'That baby is alive because she had my blood, that gives me some kind of an interest in her. Now, how is she?'

There was a pause. Then Simon said, 'Pretty good at the moment. You know there's always the chance that something will go wrong—but we're not really worrying about her at the moment.'

'Good. Now, when are you off work? I'd like to meet you.'

'I'm not sure I want to meet you,' said Simon.

Dominic took a deep breath, then decided that

Simon was entitled to feel that way. Trying to be calm, he said, 'Look, I think you have the best interests of Petra at heart. Surprisingly, so have I. So come to meet me. You can walk out whenever you feel like it.'

'All right,' Simon said slowly. 'But I do feel I'm letting Petra down a bit. I'm off in half an hour, I've got a few minutes to spare then.'

'You know the Escott Arms?' Dominic named a pub very close to the hospital. We can have a drink there.'

'I know it. See you in half an hour.'

When he'd ended the call it occurred to Dominic that he was acting like a bully. For a moment he didn't like himself. Then he realised that he didn't like not liking himself. His life was getting far too complicated.

Dominic was waiting near the entrance to the Escott Arms, an orange juice in his hand, when Simon entered. Dominic remembered the feeling of absolute fatigue that came with being an SHO. It was a job that never ended.

Neither man offered to shake hands. Dominic said, 'I owe you a favour and you look ravenous. Let me buy you a meal, they're good here.'

'There's no need. I can—.'

'There's every need. I've been an SHO myself, remember. I know what it's like. Now, I'm going to have a steak—how about you?'

'I guess I'd like a steak, too.'

So Dominic ordered, asked for a beer for Simon

and had the single glass of red wine he would allow himself. The steaks were excellent and they ate in silence. Dominic knew Simon would be more likely to open up if he wasn't hungry. Then, when they had finished, he ordered Simon another beer and a mineral water for himself.

'I don't intend to talk about my, or Petra's, private affairs. If she chooses to confide in you, that is her right. Now, she's refused all help from me. But I'm concerned that her pride is getting in the way. And I want—I intend—to do what is best for her.'

'It's a bit late for that, isn't it?' asked Simon.

'Possibly,' Dominic said, grinding his teeth. 'Now, can we concentrate on helping her and not trying to score points off each other?'

Simon thought about that. Then, reluctantly, he asked, 'What do you want to know?'

'What support has she got? Any family? Any boyfriend?'

'None of those. She was brought up by an old aunt, now she's an orphan and has literally no family. For three years she lived with someone. But he was just a parasite and it was the best thing she ever did when she ditched him. But he took all her money. Still, she has a lot of friends.'

'Has she a flat—a house?'

Simon's laugh was mirthless. 'Neither. And she'll have to move out of the nurses' home soon. Perhaps the council will house her. Or I've got a little flat, she's welcome to share that.'

'But not ideal?'

'No. Not ideal.'

Dominic thought. 'So she needs somewhere to live where she can be settled for at least a year. Has she got all the things she needs—a cot, a pram and so on?'

'I don't think so. She thought she had a few more weeks to organise things. But she was wrong.'

'Right. If she won't see me, are you willing to help her buy such things? I'll pay.'

'She doesn't need your money! I'll help her all I can but—'

'Simon! She does need my money. And if she doesn't, that tiny baby does. So I'm counting on you to persuade her to accept it. I need to see her again to sort things out. OK?'

Simon was silent a moment, then said, 'Yes, I'll persuade her to see you. When?'

'It needs to be settled soon. Tomorrow evening?'

'I'll see what I can do.'

There was silence a moment, and then Simon said, 'Do you mind if I ask a question, a personal one?'

'I might mind. But ask away and we'll see,'

'I appreciate what you're doing for Petra. And for the baby, it's the right and honourable thing to do. But are you doing it just out of a sense of duty? Is any of it because of personal feelings for her?'

Dominic took up his glass, drank the last mouthful of mineral water. It struck him that in time Simon would be an exceptional doctor, his powers of perception were great. He deserved an answer, and Dominic found he had to be honest. 'I really don't know,' he said.

*   *   *

Next day was another hard day at work for Dominic. He didn't mind, it took his mind off things. In the afternoon he found he was driving himself harder than ever. If he was working, he didn't have to think. And he didn't want to think. Not about Petra, not about the—his—baby.

Simon phoned. 'She'll see you tonight,' he said, 'but she's not very happy about it.'

'I'll be as brief as possible. Mother and child doing well?'

As well as can be expected,' said Simon. 'No great problems.' Then he rang off.

Dominic realised he was being treated as the contemptible one here. He didn't like it.

An hour later he was waiting to examine a little boy who had fallen over in the playground. An arm reached into the cubicle, grabbed him and hauled him out. 'That's a job for a junior doctor, not for you,' Susie said. 'Now, come and sit in my office and we'll have a cup of tea.'

'But, Susie, I—'

'Tea! I'm prescribing it. And one of the juniors needs the experience of working with that little devil.' Then her voice softened and she said, 'Dominic, if you get wound up much more you'll make a mistake.'

He felt the frustration raging inside him, and for a moment he was tempted to tell her that he knew what he was doing and she should keep her opinions to herself. But then he paused. He'd known Susie for over twenty years. And she could well be right. 'Perhaps I need a cup of tea,' he said, and followed Susie to the nurses' room.

'Are you going to see your baby and the girl again?' Susie asked when he had relaxed slightly.

'Yes, I'm going tonight. She said thank you for the flowers, by the way.'

'Flowers! This isn't about flowers! What are you going to do about them both?'

Susie was the only person in the hospital who would dare ask such a question. But in spite of—or perhaps because of—the twenty-five years' difference in ages, she could get away with it.

'Susie, I just don't know,' he said. 'Obviously I'll do what I have to. This baby is my—or partly my—responsibility.'

Susie snorted, and he remembered that Petra had been similarly dismissive when he'd called the baby a responsibility. 'Have you any fatherly feelings—any urge to settle down with a family?'

'Certainly not!'

'And what about this girl, Petra? How do you feel about her?'

'Well, I feel sorry for her. But, Susie, we only spent one night together. I liked her, but that was it. One night isn't much to start a relationship on.'

'Well, you certainly started something in one night. What does she think of you?'

'I don't think she likes me very much,' said Dominic. 'No, it's worse than that. She's indifferent.'

'She might think so. She might be wrong.'

He stood, went to the coffee-pot and poured himself another cup. 'Susie, I think I'm still in shock. Not two days ago I was happily looking forward to a wild night with Melanie and...this happened.'

'Melanie. Yes, Melanie phoned earlier and left a message. She'll be in touch and if you're interested, she has tonight free.'

He thought about that. Two days ago the message would have delighted him. And there would be time to see her after he'd been to see Petra. They could still have dinner, could still go for that walk along the river bank. 'I think I'll be too busy,' he said.

Petra was feeling better next day. The pain was lessening, she was no longer half-fogged by the after-effects of the anaesthetic. Her doctor was pleased with her progress. She had been down to SCBU again, held her baby, even expressed some milk for her.

Chris Fielding was there to see her, was more encouraging than before. 'Baby's doing well,' he said. 'She's going to be a fine healthy girl.' He paused and then said, 'That blood we gave her saved her life, gave her a good start.'

'I know,' Petra said coldly.

'But there are other things to worry about now. You'll have to think about what you're going to do when you're both discharged. Any plans at all?'

'I'm thinking,' she said. 'I've got one or two ideas.'

She knew Chris was concerned about Petra managing on her own. And while he knew Petra loved her baby, he was right to wonder where they would be living.

Neutrally, Chris asked, 'There's no chance of you and the father setting up home?'

She noticed he didn't call Dominic by name, even though he knew it.

'No,' she said. 'I've not been asked and I would say no if I were.'

'I see. So, do I let the council know that you're going to need accommodation?'

'We'll wait a while and then see what happens.'

But she felt desolate. She couldn't rely on the good offices of friends for ever. Soon she'd have to start planning. And it was going to be a long hard slog.

Now she was waiting to see Dominic again. She was not in the same state as she had been the night before, she was more alert, curious as to what he had to say. Simon had persuaded her to talk to Dominic, had said that she owed it to herself, her baby and even to Dominic to listen to him. So she would listen. But she wouldn't compromise.

The weather was still warm, and when he came into her room he was dressed just as he had been the day before, but this time with a blue T-shirt that emphasised his tan. He looked cool and muscular, and she felt a sudden twist of attraction. Then she felt angry. Why should he look so calm and collected while she was lying here feeling tired and in some pain?

'Simon said you just had to see me,' she snapped as soon as he came into the room. 'I agreed, but don't take too long.'

'I'm glad you agreed to see me. You're looking better, more colour to your cheeks. How are you feeling?'

'As well as anyone can after a Caesar.'

He smiled. 'Good. Those who fight back make the best patients. You'll be out of here quicker.'

He sat by her bed, pushed an expensively wrapped package towards her. 'I refused to bring more flowers. But without being asked, Susie bought these chocolates for you, then demanded that I pay her for them.'

'Thank you. Or, rather, thank her.' She put the package on her bedside table. 'Now, what have we to talk about?'

He looked at her thoughtfully. 'Simon,' he said. 'We'll talk about Simon. Do you love him?'

She looked at him horrified. 'Whatever gave you that idea?'

'Well, he obviously loves you.'

'He certainly does not. He's never even kissed me—well, not seriously. We're just very good friends.'

'He loves you,' Dominic said. 'Trust me.'

'Ought I to trust you?' she asked, and then realised that was rather unfair. She thought about what he had said. Certainly she knew that perhaps Simon would like to take their friendship a little further—but that was all. Or was it? 'Perhaps he just feels sorry for a friend and wants to help?' she offered.

'That's certainly true. But there's more to it than that.'

Petra sighed. 'I could do without this,' she said. 'The past few months I've been only concerned with myself and my baby. I've not been noticing much about what else is going on with the world. Anyway, what concern is it of yours?' A thought struck her and she said angrily, 'I suppose you think that if you can palm me off onto Simon then your own conscience will be easier.'

His face darkened and she realised he was not as imperturbable as he liked to pretend. She felt slightly nervous. But when he spoke his voice was as calm as ever.

'My conscience concerns only me. And I think enough of you not to want to palm you off onto anyone.'

'Sorry,' she muttered, and then wondered why she had to apologise to him.

'And I can't say I really like Simon but I respect him and I think he'll be a good doctor. A girl could do a lot worse than him.'

'Could we stop talking about Simon? I'm getting rather tired.'

'Of course.' His face grew neutral again. 'Now, I extracted from him the fact that you have no family, no home, no savings.'

'That was personal! And it's no business of yours. I'll cope somehow.'

'I'm sure you will. Now, I am unmarried, unattached, I'm paid very well and I bank much of it because there's nothing I want to spend it on.'

'Bully for you.'

He ignored that. 'I want to find you a flat or a house and rent it for you, for a year at first. I want to give you money for furniture and a pram and cot and all the things you need for a baby. And I intend to give you an allowance.'

'Why?'

'Because you need it. And because I've never backed away from my responsibilities. And I suppose you could take me to court and get money that way.'

'I'd never do that!'

He looked at her curiously. 'I knew you'd say that. Anyway, it doesn't signify. I want and intend to pay.'

'Dominic, I want nothing from you. Because you're nothing to me.'

She saw him staring at her and she couldn't work out what his expression meant. A small smile—it almost seemed like reluctant admiration. But then his face became completely neutral. He said, 'Petra, you have a responsibility to your child. Whatever you feel for or about me, you can't let your pride stand in the way of the welfare of the baby. You'd be punishing her to please yourself.'

There was a long silence this time. She didn't know quite how she felt. Differing emotions warred inside her. There was anger at being forced into this position. There was reluctant admiration for his stand. And there was a vague wish that he'd offer to do something for her because he wanted to—not because his sense of duty made him. She hated being obligated. Eventually, she said, 'All right. Thank you for your generous offer. I'm accepting, not for myself but for my baby.'

'I realise that.' There was another silence.

'Will you visit us to see your child?' she asked after a while. She emphasised the 'your.' She wanted this man to suffer.

After a while he said, 'I believe children should be planned, wanted and hoped for, not come as accidents.'

'I'll take that as a no, then,' she said. He left shortly afterwards.

Petra felt uneasy. She had to acknowledge that his offer had been generous in the extreme, and that her own future now looked a lot brighter than before. So why did she still feel dissatisfied? He unsettled her. Every time he came, he unsettled her. Her life was in a mess and every time he came she had flashes of memory of that night they had spent together. It had been so marvellous. And the consequences had been so disastrous. Then she realised that she was thinking of her daughter as a disaster, and felt ashamed.

She reached for the package he had brought her, stripped aside the wrapping paper. A very expensive box of chocolates. Good, she would enjoy them. Pulling aside the Cellophane, she found that it had been slit and an envelope slid inside. She opened the envelope to find a congratulations card. There was a message. He's not all that bad. May I see the baby some time? Congratulations, Susie Cash. Then there was a telephone number.

Petra blinked. For a moment she had hoped that the card had come from Dominic.

It was two days later. It was quite like old times. Old times? Had it been only a week since she had been one of this team?

She had been taken again down to SCBU to see her baby. But when she got there there was that atmosphere of controlled excitement that she remembered so well. 'Remember Baby Rathbone?' Erica asked her. 'You nursed her—in fact, you were the first one to guess that she'd got RDS.'

'That's right! Chris decided that it might not be too serious, but that we'd keep a close eye on her.'

RDS—respiratory distress syndrome—sometimes developed in a baby whose lungs were just not strong enough to manage on their own. And sometimes it developed because the baby couldn't produce enough surfactant—the substance that coated the insides of the air sacs in the lungs.

'Well, it's got worse,' Erica said. 'Definite lack of surfactant. Skin got mottled, those blue membranes inside her mouth, just not getting enough oxygen, even with the mask on. So Chris is going to give her some surfactant.'

This was a highly specialised operation, involving allowing the thick liquid to enter the windpipe and make its slow way into the lungs.

'Do you think I could watch? I get bored just lying in bed and I miss the work.'

'Of course you can watch.' Chris's voice came from behind her. 'Baby Rathbone owes you a lot. Just keep to the side of the room.'

So she watched as, with Erica's help, Chris introduced the tube and slowly fed in the liquid. Then the baby was given extra air and oxygen, using a ventilator. It was precise, exacting work and it thrilled her to watch. She had been part of this team. In time she would be again.

It was interesting. And different. Now she had one of those tiny bits of humanity herself. She was surprised at how much it altered her view of things.

Afterwards she went to see her baby and was sitting there watching her and expressing her milk at the same time. It seemed to come easier. And there was endless fascination in watching the little movements of her daughter.

There was a cough behind her, and she turned. To her surprise she saw Dominic. 'Oh, I'm sorry,' he said when he saw what she was doing. 'I'll wait till you've finished and—'

'There's no need. I'm sure you've seen milk being expressed before.' Then, because she was feeling happy, she teased him and said, 'And anyway, it's not as if you haven't seen my breasts before.'

'Quite.' He looked shocked, then rallied and said, 'I see you're feeling better.'

'No use moping. And things are looking up for me.'

He came further into the room and she saw his face properly. There was a great bruise down one cheek, from the eye to the corner of his mouth. 'What happened to your face?' she asked, horrified. 'That's a terrible bruise.'

He shrugged. 'Just one of the chances you take in A and E. I was called in last night. Police brought in a man high on drugs and alcohol. He'd got into a fight and was complaining of pain in his abdomen. We got him onto a trolley, I turned away and when I turned back he lashed out, caught me here. My fault, I should have known. Never trust a drunk on drugs.'

'It's not like that in SCBU,' she said. 'Well, not usually.' There had been a couple of cases in which parents had had too much to drink.

'The joke is,' Dominic went on, 'I found he had a

ruptured spleen. We removed it. Perhaps I saved his life.'

'Always exciting,' she said. She was a little upset at how distressed she had felt when seeing the bruise. She knew A and E staff were in constant danger of assault. Why should it worry her so much that Dominic had been hit?

He had walked over to the incubator, was studying her baby—their baby—his face unreadable. 'Baby doing fine?' he asked.

'Improving. Getting stronger. We're all very pleased with her progress.'

Good. When will you be able to hold her?'

'Soon,' she said. 'In fact, probably now, if I insisted. But I'll wait until everyone is absolutely certain it's all right.' She tried to look at him, hold his gaze, and said, 'Would you like to hold her?'

He avoided eye contact. 'Perhaps. In time, perhaps. But, really, I called to say I've been to a couple of estate agents, found the addresses of a number of flats that are both pleasant and convenient. I thought you might like to have a look through them, see what you think.'

She took the leaflets that he offered her, started to look through them. There were some rather lovely places. Then she caught sight of the price of one of them. Involuntarily, she caught her breath. 'They're rather a lot of money!'

'I can afford them. That's not your worry.'

His face was stern as he spoke to her and it angered her. 'I won't worry. You made an offer, I accepted. When we're in a flat, will you call sometimes to visit your child?' She could see that he knew that she was deliberately trying to irritate him.

But he remained calm. 'I might,' he said.

His calmness angered her more. 'When I'm better, when I've recovered. Would you call because you'd expect sex from me as a kind of payment?'

He looked at her and she shivered when she saw the anger on his face. He said, 'I deserve a lot but I don't deserve that. The answer, if you want one, is no.'

She felt ashamed. 'I'm sorry,' she said. 'You're being very good to me—to us. Put it down to baby blues.'

'We'll forget it. Have you got a list of the things you will need for the baby? Doesn't the hospital or someone give you some idea of what you should buy?'

'I know what I'll need. After all this is my speciality.'

'Hmm. In that case, shall I just give you a cheque to start things off? I'd like to think things were moving, I've got to go to Amsterdam for a conference for five days and I just cannot miss it.'

'We'll talk about things when you come back,' she said. 'I won't need any money till then. The baby won't be discharged in the next five days and if I'm discharged I still have my room in the nurses' home.'

'Fair enough. But I'll leave you a cheque anyway and if possible I would like a decision on the flat.'

She had been skimming though the leaflets, she pointed to one. 'I really like this one. I've got friends nearby and it's in a lovely position.'

'Good. Then I'll set things in motion. I'll lease it for a year and then we can review the situation.'

'It might be a situation to you,' she said, 'but to me it's my life.'

'Yes. I'm sorry.' And then she thought that just for once he revealed a bit of himself. 'I find this all easier to deal with if we stick to practicalities and forget about emotions.'

'I'm sure you do. But my emotions have to be involved. You can't be a good parent and not love your child.'

He was walking restlessly round the room, peering at equipment, opening and closing doors. His back was to her, but when she mentioned parents' loving their child, she saw his shoulders stiffen. She had upset him.

You must be getting tired of people referring to Baby Morgan,' he said after a while. 'Have you thought of a name yet?'

'On the birth certificate she will be known as Morgan.'

He flinched again but didn't comment. 'I meant first names,' he said.

She smiled to herself. She had spent a happy hour last night chatting to a nurse friend, trying to decide on a name. 'I've narrowed it down to three. Eleanor, Chloe and Charlotte. They all go well with Morgan, don't they?'

Dominic had turned to face her and she was suddenly dismayed at the sadness on his face. 'Don't you like them?' she asked.

At first he didn't reply. Then he said, 'I have no

rights, it's your choice, your baby. But I would like it if you didn't call her Charlotte.'

'Well, I haven't made up my mind yet, but what have you got against Charlotte?'

He shrugged, he was in control again now. 'Nothing at all. Sheer prejudice. You must make up your own mind.'

Petra thought he was lying—but why?

A few moments later, he left.

Dominic walked rapidly across the hospital car park, got in his car and slammed the door. He drove as fast as he could through the grounds then sped inland along the fortunately quiet road. Then after a while he forced himself to slow down. Was there anything he despised more than people who drove too fast because they were upset? He took a side road, drove up into the Wolds. Then he stopped. Time to think.

He thought he had been coping with this situation pretty well. As well as it could be coped with. But now the name Charlotte had upset him. He had thought it was something he was over—evidently not. The pain was still there. And this newborn baby was bringing it out again.

In future he would have to work harder than ever at keeping his distance from the child. Looking her had been… Well, he decided he had felt what any normal person would feel. Awe, tenderness…love of a kind? Nothing to do with him being the baby's father. Nothing at all.

It struck him that he had been thinking almost entirely about the baby. What about Petra? She was the one suffering most. How did he feel about her? So far she had just been the mother of the baby who had come along to spoil his life. He realised that he had put off thinking about her because he didn't want to examine his own feelings too closely. He would have to think about her. She was a person in her own right.

Sex with Petra had been mind-blowing. They had fitted so well together, each knowing what the other needed and had to give. She had also been fun to be with. Talking to her had been interesting, stimulating. She was a good companion.

It would have been so easy to get in touch with her. But he hadn't. He had sensed that capacity in her, that willingness to give. That need for love. And he hadn't wanted this. He had only wanted relationships without commitment. He still only wanted relationships without commitment. So he hadn't phoned Petra.

Now he was wondering. Was his attitude a bit juvenile? A bit shallow? And if it was—what had he given up?

He didn't know.

CHAPTER FOUR

'HE'S been to see you again?' asked Simon.

Petra nodded. She was back in her bed, a little tired and perhaps a bit bewildered by what was happening to her. Simon was visiting and it was good just to lie there, having a relaxed conversation.

She hadn't told him about Dominic's offer, and she had hidden the details of the flat she had decided on. Of course, Simon probably knew. But at the moment she didn't want to talk to him about it. She wanted to think a bit more about Dominic.

She had to think about Simon too. Dominic had said Simon was in love with her. She hoped he only thought he was.

'Dominic says he wants to do the right thing,' she said. 'I suppose I can respect him for that.'

'I've asked around about him,' Simon went on, his voice rather hoarse. 'He's got a very good reputation as a doctor. He gets all the difficult cases in A and E. He's fast and he's efficient but he won't take risks. If you're injured in a motor accident, hope to get him looking at you.'

'I know a lot of good doctors,' she said. 'I think you're one. What else did you find out? What about his personal life?'

'He's a supposed to be a bit of a womaniser,' Simon said flatly.

'Surprise me,' she said. 'That's enough about Dominic. Tell me about you. You said you had something important to ask me.'

He looked uncomfortable. 'Sort of. I've been offered a two-month course down in London and I'm going on it. You know I've got a little flat in Denham?'

She grinned. 'You've told me about it. Very little, you said.'

'It is. But I won't be using it for a couple of months, and I wondered—just to get you started—if you'd like to move in. Then when I came back we could…well, we could see… Just as a friend, of course.'

She leaned forward, pulled his head towards her and kissed his cheek. 'Simon, that's a wonderful offer and I'm so touched. But it isn't necessary. It's arranged. I'm moving into a flat.'

'Oh. That's good.'

She could see he was disappointed so she said, 'You will be visiting us while you're on this course, won't you? You'll come and see me and the baby?'

'Of course I will. Look forward to it. Have you thought of a name for her yet?'

'I thought Eleanor.'

'I like it. Any special—?'

A nurse put her head round the door. 'Petra, you've got another visitor. He says he must see you, that you'll want to see him, and that it's good news.'

'Show him in, then. I need all the good news I can get.'

'I'd better go,' muttered Simon. 'I'm still on duty.

Call to see you later.' He looked thoughtfully at the man who entered as he left, but said nothing.

Petra thought he looked rather a nice man. He had a dark suit, a briefcase, a pleasant smile.

'Ms Petra Morgan? Formerly at the Villa, 18 Parkway, and then at 74 Medlar Road and last of all the nurses' home here at the hospital?'

'That's me,' Petra said. 'Those are my last three addresses. Why do you want to know?'

'May I sit down? I think I have some good news for you.'

Dominic had a good conference in Amsterdam. It was on new techniques in the golden hour—the name given to the first hour after a person was seriously injured. In this hour decisions were often made that could determine whether the patient would live or die. There were lectures and discussions on resuscitation, on emergency care outside the department. He decided that he would put some of the ideas into practice in his own department—and when he became consultant...

There was a social life as well. It was good to gossip in the bar with colleagues. And he met Anna again. Six-foot-tall, red-headed Anna. She was an A and E consultant from Chicago—or rather an ER consultant as they are called in the States. They had met three years previously at a similar conference and had got on rather well.

They had a drink in the bar and she told him she was now divorced. Then he took her out to dinner. It was a pleasant evening and he enjoyed her company.

But when they returned to their hotel he didn't try to take things any further. Even when she showed her obvious disappointment.

This worried him. He decided that Petra and her baby were taking up too much of his attention.

As soon as he had arrived at the hotel he had phoned SCBU with his number, had asked Chris Fielding to let him know if there was any alteration in the baby's health. He explained he was very ready to give more blood if it was necessary. Chris had drily said that it was not very likely but thanked him for the offer.

On the plane flying back to Manchester he found that he was rather looking forward to seeing the baby again. Of course he would keep his distance. But he thought he might take up Petra's offer, and drop in at the flat to see the baby. Just occasionally. Then he remember Petra's angry accusation—did he expect sex in return for any kindness? The thought of sex with Petra threw his mind into a turmoil, he just couldn't cope with it.

When he arrived back at his department he showed Susie what he had bought—a white silk and lace christening gown. He spread it open to show her.

It's beautiful,' Susie said, feeling the filigree lace. 'You're getting there slowly.'

'Getting where?' he asked, but didn't wait for a reply.

As expected, things had piled up in his absence. There was a pile of letters to be answered, administrative problems to be worked out. He worked a night shift, had a few hours' sleep, then drove over to Denham to the hospital. He'd call on Petra first and then go to see the baby.

He knew Petra was still in hospital but due to be discharged shortly. They had things to discuss—he had to set her up in the flat, make sure she had all that she needed. He had made arrangements about the flat before he'd left, but there would certainly be things to sign. He'd be seeing quite a bit of her over the next few days. And a distant part of his mind told him that he was looking forward to it. Just a bit.

When he looked into her side ward he was surprised to see that Petra had a visitor. There was a man sitting by her bed and the bed was covered with papers. Petra appeared to be signing something.

She looked up when he tapped on the door. A smile flashed across her face. 'Hi, Dominic, hope you had a good conference. I'm a bit busy now. Why don't you go to see Eleanor and then come back in, say, half an hour?'

She glanced at the man by her bedside who nodded and said, 'Half an hour will be fine to wrap this up.'

'All right,' said Dominic. In fact, he couldn't see Eleanor, he'd called at SCBU first and it wasn't convenient for a while.

He walked out into the summer sun. He felt that he'd just been dismissed. He wasn't sure that he liked this new, confident Petra. He had an uneasy feeling that things were going to change, that they were out of his control. Who was that man and what were the papers?

He returned in exactly half an hour—timed to the minute.

He saw that the man was still with Petra but the papers were now stowed in his briefcase. The man shook hands with Petra and said, 'It all seems very satisfactory. But I'll come back to you in a couple of days and we'll see how the figures work out exactly.'

'Thank you, Mr Grimley,' Petra said. 'You've been a real help.'

The man left, smiling politely at Dominic, and hesitantly Dominic entered and sat by the bed. What was going on?

'It's good to see you, Dominic,' said Petra. 'Come and tell me all about the conference. Did you learn a lot?'

This was a completely new Petra. Of course she had recovered from her Caesarean, she was less pale, looked more like the tremendously attractive woman he had first met. But there was more to it than that. Her eyes sparkled. She was more confident, more serene. And it made him feel less confident.

'It was worthwhile,' he said, and then pushed the package he had brought over to her. 'I was just passing a place—I thought you might like this.'

She opened the package, took out the christening robe. 'Dominic, this is lovely!' She leaned out of bed, kissed him on the cheek.

It was the first time she had kissed him since... since that night. It was meant to be just a friendly, thank-you kiss. So he was surprised at how much it set his pulse racing.

'I'll see you're invited to the christening,' she said. 'Incidentally, I'm going to call the baby Eleanor.'

'Nice name,' he said, 'but you told me before. Eleanor...Morgan. Sounds good.'

'I've got some good news for you,' she said, 'some really good news. You didn't want this baby, did you? It came as a shock. You told me that babies should be planned so you didn't want this one, did you?'

'Well, no,' he said, 'not really. It was a shock. If you had got in touch with me before, I—'

'It doesn't matter now. I have to say that I was really impressed by your offer of the flat and the money and the allowance. It was kind of you, and honourable and generous. But now it's not necessary. I don't need the money.'

He looked at her blankly. 'You don't need the money?'

'Not a penny. A man came to visit me while you were away. A bit of a shock, but the nicest man I've seen in a long time.' She paused and smiled, obviously relishing the tension she was building up.

'For years I've had a hundred pounds invested in Premium Bonds. I'd never won anything. But suddenly I have, and it's a considerable sum of money.'

'Congratulations,' croaked Dominic. He couldn't think what else to say.

Petra went on, 'I won't need your rented flat now; I'm buying one in the same block. I hope you don't mind, Mr Grimley cancelled all the arrangements you'd kindly made.

'I've spent a bit of money on furnishings and things for the baby. And I've had professional advice from

Mr Grimley on how to invest the rest of the money to provide an income. Eleanor and I are now completely independent. We can look after ourselves.'

From a folder by her bed she took a cheque, he recognised it as the one he had given her. She gave to him. 'Thanks again, Dominic. But this is goodbye.'

He was used to dealing with shocks in A and E. No matter how serious a case might be, it was important to keep a steady face, not to let your emotions show. But this was too much of a shock.

'Really goodbye? Not see each other again?'

'Well, we might bump into each other occasionally. I gather your A and E department is moving here in six months or so. But otherwise we're back to the situation when you didn't know about the baby. Forget us both.'

'But I do know about her now! I just can't forget. And…anyway you've invited me to the christening.' Even to himself it sounded feeble.

'You can come if you want. But you never wanted a baby, did you? Well, not an unexpected one, you made that quite clear. When you found out you were horrified. And now you don't have to do anything for us at all. Go back to your old happy carefree life. I thought you'd be pleased.'

'Well, yes. It just takes a bit of getting used to.' He thought for a minute. 'But what about you and me?'

'There is no you and me,' she said. 'Just a memory.'

Eleanor had been born at thirty-two weeks. If all went well she might be discharged from SCBU at thirty-five weeks. Petra was discharged from her ward after ten days. She had another eleven days to prepare a home for her daughter.

It was important not to try to do too much. For a while she moved back into the nurses' home, rested when she was told to. But planning and supplying was so much fun!

Mr Grimley had worked wonders with the flat. He had suggested that she rent for a year with the option to buy at the end of that time. She could look round, think about her future. Petra agreed, just so long as she'd be able to move in a couple of days before she brought Eleanor home. And now she needed furnishings.

Never before in her life had Petra had money to spend on whatever she liked. It was so nice to be able to pick clothes without having to first looking at the price. It was so nice to buy a brand-new pram, carrycot, layette. But old habits died hard. She didn't overspend—the money was for Eleanor's future.

A few days after she'd said goodbye to Dominic, when she'd just moved back into the nurses' home, she received a letter. It wasn't a handwriting she recognised, but the deep black ink, the bold strokes of the letters, made her guess. This was the kind of forceful handwriting she'd expect from Dominic.

She sat on the bed to open her letter, her heart perhaps thumping a little more than usual. Inside was a postcard—a picture of a Monet garden. On the other side it read, Congratulations again on your win. However, I do still feel some sense of responsibility towards Eleanor. When you move into your new flat would it be possible for me to visit there, just to make sure everything is well? If you agree, could you let me know the address and telephone number? All good wishes, Dominic.

Not exactly a love letter, she thought. Well, he could have her address. On impulse she phoned the A and E department at Calthorpe.

'Would it be possible to speak to Dr Tate, if he's there?' she asked the pleasant-voiced nurse who answered the phone. 'My name is Petra Morgan.'

'Petra! I feel I know you. I'm Susie Cash, the ward manager here. And I'm a friend of Dominic's.'

'Oh, yes. You sent the flowers. And that little note about seeing Eleanor. That was very kind of you.'

'It was nothing. I'd still like to see the baby.'

'Why?' asked Petra. 'Dominic doesn't seem very keen on seeing her.'

Susie laughed. 'Don't you believe it. But give him time. Mostly, he doesn't know what he wants himself. I've known Dominic since he was fifteen. He's been restless but he'll settle down. Incidentally, have you two had a row?'

'There's nothing to row about,' said Petra, a bit surprised. 'We've got nothing in common now. He ought to be happy, I've just told him that I don't need any support from him.'

'Well, happy he is not. Working with him over the past few days has been hell. No one can do anything right, he's been a devil with the staff. It's a good thing we all love him.'

'Love him? You do?' It struck her that, apart from

Simon's reluctant appraisal, this was the first time anyone had said anything positive about Dominic. In fact, this was the first time she had spoken to someone who liked him.

'We do. He's a good boss—most of the time. Never too busy to stop and explain something to a junior. And a brilliant doctor.'

'Yes, I've heard that. It's just some of the other sides of his character...'

She heard Susie sigh. 'Don't tell me. I know. But I do think— She's what?'

Petra guessed that the sudden exclamation was not directed at her. Dimly she could hear an exchange between a semi-hysterical voice and Susie's calmer tones. Then Susie came back on the line.

'Work calls. Got to go, Petra. Someone is haemorrhaging. To answer your question, you can't talk to Dominic, he's been called out on a RTA. Shall I get him to call you back?'

'No need, Susie. But could you give him this address? I'll be in it in a week or so.'

She gave the address and rang off. She had liked Susie and was puzzled. Why was Dominic in such a bad temper? He should have been pleased that he was free of any ties whatsoever. It just didn't make sense.

She didn't hear anything more from Dominic. In fact, she was too busy to think about him, she had her home to move into, to organise. And then a week later she was allowed to take Eleanor home.

'I know Eleanor has the best nurse in the world,' Chris told her, 'but, remember, she's still a prem. Any doubt, any problem, we want to know at once.'

Petra was kangaroo nursing. She looked down at the tiny head nestling between her breasts. 'This baby couldn't have had a better start in life than being nursed here,' she said. 'I know that. You'll all come to visit us?'

'Try to keep us away,' said Chris.

So she moved into her own home. Her very own home. She'd decided on a ground-floor, garden flat. From her living room she could see through her French windows onto a little patio and her own small patch of greenery. When Eleanor was bigger it would be a lovely place for her to play.

It was now her second evening in the flat. Eleanor was sleeping in her pram on the patio. Petra sat in her wooden chair, gently rocking and thinking about how her life had changed.

She thought she should have been perfectly happy, contented. But she wasn't…quite. She believed that the perfect upbringing for a child included both a mother and a father. She herself had had neither. She had been brought up by an old maiden aunt who had done what she could but who had never quite managed to understand Petra.

Petra smiled grimly to herself. Eleanor would do better.

It had been a busy time but she was settled now and she had time to think. She could think about Dominic. There had been so much excitement and worry over the past few weeks that she had not had time to wonder exactly what he was feeling. She realised he was rather an enigma.

The night she had spent with him had been magic.

Nothing before in her life had prepared her for the rapture he had brought her. And what had made it better was the fact that she had thought he had felt the same way. Their joy had been mutual.

He had told her honestly that there had been no future for them and she had accepted that—at the time. But then she had wondered if he might get in touch. But he hadn't. And when that hope had faded she had resigned herself. At least she had had one night.

Then she had found out she had been pregnant. She had decided at once not to tell him. She had made the mistake. It would be hard enough bringing up a child, she didn't want the additional problem of having to deal with a man who felt he had been unfairly trapped.

She had been unfair to him. He had been entitled to know. And she should have guessed that he was an honourable man, would have wanted to do the right thing by her. And that was the problem. He would have done the right thing by her out of duty, out of a sense of obligation.

He wouldn't have helped her out of love. And love was what she wanted. She knew, she had known all along, that Dominic didn't, couldn't love her. And now, though she was happy, the tears slid down her face. Not because of Dominic, of course. She was still emotional, her hormones were still in turmoil. She wasn't worried about Dominic at all. She knew she didn't love him.

She stood and made herself a cup of tea. The universal remedy. And when she had drunk it, she felt better.

CHAPTER FIVE

IT WAS good to live in her flat with her baby. She had everything she needed—she shuddered to think of what life would have been like without her windfall, even with Dominic's help. She had bought herself some badly needed new clothes and was now wearing an attractive tracksuit kind of outfit that was fashionable, smart and easy to clean. The last was important.

She had decided not to let herself go, like some of the mothers she had seen. For her there was no excuse. So, even though it was an effort, she kept her hair neat and a touch of make-up always on her face. It made her feel better.

And there were always friends dropping in, just to see that she was all right and offering to help.

Her doorbell rang, probably another friend. She needed a friend to chat to for a while, to take her mind off things. So she smiled as she opened the door. Then her smile turned to a grimace of horror. On the doorstep was Ken Bannister—her one-time lover.

He smiled at her. 'Hello, Petra, good to see you. Not inviting me in?' He lifted an ill-wrapped parcel. 'I've brought a few of your things, you left them behind.'

Before she knew what was happening he was in the flat, closing the door behind him. He looked round appreciatively. 'You're doing well, Petra, this is a nice flat.'

From somewhere she found her voice. 'What do you want?'

'I wanted to see you. We go back a long way, we can't forget that in a hurry, can we?'

She looked at him, as if seeing him for the first time. She hadn't seen him for nearly a year. She used to think of him as good-looking, well dressed. Now she saw him as he was—seedy, with unwashed hair and untidy clothes. He was never dressed like that when he was with me, she thought with a little touch of satisfaction. He had deteriorated.

She didn't like it when he sat in one of her arm-chairs without asking. 'Thanks for bringing my stuff,' she said, 'but I must ask you to go now. I'm just about to feed the baby.' It was a lie, but she wanted him out of her flat as quickly as possible.

He didn't move. 'Don't mind me, just carry on,' he said. 'Is there any chance of a cup of tea?'

'No. You're not staying.'

She knew that this was a new Petra talking. She wouldn't have spoken to him like that before.

His face darkened, obviously he was not used to this new Petra. And he didn't much like her. 'We used to be close,' he said, 'we shared everything. Now I hear you've done rather well for yourself.'

Then she understood. 'You want money,' she said.

He looked at her with apparent horror. How well she remembered that false expression. 'That was the last thing on my mind,' he said, 'though if you want to invest there's a couple of projects you might be interested in. There's a place up on the moors that I—'

'Just get out, Ken!' she snarled. She felt enraged. All right, it might be the result of hormones but still she felt enraged. Who did he think he was?

A project she might be interested in? How dared he treat her as he had and then expect her to believe that line?

'I fell for your sweet-talking once before,' she said, 'but never again. Get back to Karen. The two of you deserve each other.'

His face grew even angrier but she saw him trying to control his rage. 'Karen's gone,' he said. 'I know now that you're the only woman for me and that we both made a mistake. But if we got together again I think that we—'

She laughed. 'No power on earth could make me get together again with you, Ken. To think I spent three years with you! I should have known what you were like after three minutes.'

He saw that she meant it and decided to change tack. 'Well, I'm not very happy. I gather you won with money that you earned while living with me. Those were our joint earnings and I'm entitled to half. I've been in touch with my solicitor and he says—'

Now she was even more enraged. 'Your solicitor? Which bar did you meet him in?'

He leaped to his feet in a fury but her only concern was for Eleanor. He shouted, 'I'm telling you half that money's mine and I won't leave here until—' The doorbell rang.

'Leave it!' he said, but she evaded his outstretched hand and ran to the door.

It was Dominic. And instantly she knew that things would be all right.

'Dominic! I'm so glad to see you! There's someone here. I've got to—'

'I know. I could hear from outside the door.' He put his arm round her shoulders, warm and comforting. 'Let's go and sort things out,' he said.

They entered the living room together. Dominic said nothing, just stared at Ken. Petra looked from one man to the other. There was a contrast. Dominic was in his usual T-shirt and chinos. Ken wore a flashy, none-too-clean Hawaiian-type shirt and grubby trousers. Dominic had the narrow waist, broad shoulders. Ken was getting slightly fat.

Ken tried blustering. He said, 'This is a private conversation, so why don't you leave and—?'

Dominic walked forward so that Ken had to walk backwards until he was pinned against the wall. The two men's heads were only inches apart. And Dominic said, very softly, 'I came here to see my child. I don't like seeing you in the same flat as her, I don't like seeing you anywhere. You can get out of here now, unharmed. But if I hear that you've called, or tried to get in touch again by any means, then you'll be in trouble. Understand?'

'You can't talk to me like that,' Ken quavered. 'I've got rights…'

Petra blinked. She had never seen anything like it. Dominic put his hands under Ken's arms and lifted him bodily off the floor. Ken's feet were dangling. 'I am talking to you like that,' Dominic said, 'and I'll talk to you any way I want. Now get out or I won't be responsible for the consequences.'

He dropped Ken. Petra heard the thud as his feet hit the ground. Ken looked lost. Dominic took him by the arm and led him to the door. Petra heard the door shut. And suddenly she was shivering.

Dominic returned, looked at her assessingly. 'He's gone,' he said. 'I take it that was the ex-boyfriend?'

'Very ex-boyfriend,' Petra managed to say. She was finding it difficult to talk. Ken's visit had upset her far more than she had thought possible.

'You don't look too good. I'll fetch you some tea.' Dominic took her by the hand, led her to her couch. There was a blanket at one end of it, which he threw over her. Even though it was a warm day she found it comforting.

'I don't want any tea, not for a minute. Just sit here with me.'

She realised that he knew what she wanted. She wanted, needed, comfort and reassurance. So he sat by her and put his arm round her shoulders. She leaned against him. She could feel the warmth of his body, caught a hint of his now familiar spicy after-shave. She liked this. Just for a while she could relax here without thinking, content just to be there.

'Where's Eleanor?'

'She's asleep on the patio,' Petra said drowsily, and nodded in the direction of the open French windows. 'You can see her in a minute.' Then she closed her eyes.

Of course, it couldn't last. He seemed quite content

to sit with her in silence but it couldn't last. After a while she said, 'Did you mention tea?'

Gently he removed his arm from round her, looked at her in that doctor-like way. He took her wrist, felt her pulse. 'You heart was beating like a kettledrum before,' he said, 'but it's more or less normal now. Did he upset you much?'

'I can cope, he's not a big problem. And, surprisingly, I seem to have got stronger recently.'

'I suspect you've always been strong. You just didn't know it. I'll make the tea, and may I see Eleanor?'

'Certainly go to look. But don't disturb her, I could do with a few minutes' peace.' Then she frowned. 'Why do you want to see her?'

'Just curious. I thought I might drop in just for a minute. You said I could.'

'I remember,' she said. She couldn't quite work out what Dominic's attitude was. He had been perfectly happy dealing with Ken. Now he seemed unsure of himself.

He found his way to the kitchen and she heard him fill the kettle. Then he came out and went onto the patio. She could see the long line of the cream chinos stretched against his calves and thighs, see his bent back as he peered into the pram. He seemed to be longer than a minute looking down at Eleanor. Then he came back and went to the kitchen. The kettle had been boiled for quite a time.

He put a tray on the coffee-table and sat by her side on the couch again. But he didn't put his arm round her. He had found her chocolate biscuits, she noted. Good. She needed a bit of instant energy. Together, in silence, they drank tea and ate biscuits. She felt they were happy, companionable together.

'I take it he was trying to extract money from you?'

'You bet he was. And he won't get a penny!' She was still surprised at her own anger. 'I can see him for what he is now. A mean, pointless scrounger. To think that for all those years I lived with him, gave him my money, looked after him. How could I have been so stupid to...?' To her horror she found tears coming to her eyes again.

He moved closer, put his arm round her again and held her close to him. It was so comforting. 'I know what you mean,' he said. 'There have been times I've done things...wondered afterwards how I could have done that. It happens, I know.'

Petra looked at him curiously. His face was bleak. Somehow she had reminded him of something out of his own past. Something he was not very happy with.

'What was it? Are you going to tell me about it?' she asked.

Dominic shook his head. 'I'm just thinking generally,' he said. 'Nothing really specific.'

But she didn't believe him and she could have smiled at the quick way he tried to change the subject. 'Are you feeling better now?' he asked.

'A lot better. Dominic, you should know, this is just baby blues. I'm highly emotional because my hormones are all over the place. It's a common complaint. We see it in mothers all the time at the unit. It'll pass in a day or two.'

'Feelings are real whether they're brought on by hormones or not.'

True.' She had finished her tea, eaten her biscuits and now she felt fatigue beating at her. 'I like your arm being round me,' she said sleepily. 'I like it but I know it isn't sex. I don't even think I like you very much. This is comfort, and I do like that.'

'So do I,' he said. 'And I'm sorry you don't like me very much. I do have one or two good points.'

'Some day you can tell me about them.' She didn't really want to carry on with this conversation, she was tired. She didn't want to have to think. So she said, 'I was up at half past three this morning, and so now I'm a bit sleepy. Looking after a baby is hard work.'

'I know that. In fact, I'm a bit sleepy too. I've been up since five myself. Got called in—they couldn't quite cope in A and E.'

He leaned closer to her, she could feel him studying her face. 'You must be uncomfortable, leaning on me like this. Why don't you go and lie on the bed for a while? I'll watch Eleanor.'

She wasn't uncomfortable, but the thought of bed for a few minutes was wonderful. 'Sounds good,' she said.

She allowed him to ease her to her feet, lead her to the bedroom. There she kicked off her shoes and collapsed onto the bed. Her eyes closed at once. This was bliss! She heard him walk away quietly, leaving the bedroom door slightly ajar. That way she would hear if Eleanor cried out.

For a few minutes she dozed. Then she realised she couldn't sleep. There was something nagging at her but she wasn't sure what. Something she hadn't done, wanted to do, ought to do. What was it?

And where was Dominic? What was he doing? There was complete silence from the room next door. 'What are you doing?' she called irritably. 'I want to know what you're doing.'

'I'm babysitting,' came the calm voice from outside. 'In fact, I'm doing more than that. I'm baby-looking.'

He appeared in her bedroom again. 'She's growing,' he said. 'She's still a tiny baby but she's growing.'

He came further into the room, sat on the bed. Well, he had to, there were no bedside chairs. He took her hand.

'Don't you dare take my pulse again,' she said. 'I've had enough of you being a doctor for a while.'

She thought he was going to drop her hand, so she said, 'But you can hold it if you want.'

So he did. For some reason she thought it would be easier for her to sleep now. And she could tell by the deepening of Dominic's breathing that he was near sleep too. But he must be uncomfortable, sitting there. So she edged to the side of the bed, and pulled him down by her. 'Don't say anything, just sleep,' she muttered.

He lay there. He didn't touch her but he didn't let go of her hand. It was what she wanted. This was nothing. They weren't even friends. But for a while this could be a little interlude in their lives.

Perhaps for a few minutes she did sleep. But then she found herself waking up. There was a man by her

side, a man who had one been—possibly still was—
attracted to her. Everything they both had done in the
past few minutes, the way they came to be lying together, seemed entirely reasonable. Though she knew
other people wouldn't think so.

He was still holding her hand.

She opened her eyes, turned her head towards him.
He must have felt the little motion as she saw his
eyes open, too. There was a second's silent commu-
nion. She knew what he wanted and she wanted it
too.

She closed her eyes and leaned a little towards him.
When he touched his lips to hers she put her arm
round his neck, he put his arm round her waist.

At first the kiss was gentle. She knew that he was
hesitant, not knowing what she—or he—really
wanted. Then the kiss grew deeper. They pulled towards each other, tasting each other's sweetness. She
eased her body towards his, letting her breasts rest
against him, becoming aware of his need for her.
After two ecstatic moments like this she rolled onto
her back, pulling him with her. She wanted more.

His hand was on her blouse, unbuttoning the front,
revealing her nursing bra. 'Sorry,' she mumbled. 'Not
a very sexy garment, is it? You must think I look a
mess.'

'I think you look marvellous,' he said hoarsely, and
then his lips were on hers.

Now his hand was at her waist, trailed lower, she
felt a little shock as his fingers touched the end of her
Ceasarean scar. He knew at once what it was and his

hand jerked back. Then he sat upright. And suddenly the atmosphere changed.

'What are we doing?' he asked, his voice horrified. 'This is madness!'

She felt the dreariness of her previous mood return. 'Just hormones,' she quoted back at him. 'They run riot, every new mother suffers from it. Nothing to worry about.'

He didn't like her flippant words. 'Yes, but…this nearly was a terrible mistake, Petra! We've already made one and—'

'Don't call my daughter a mistake!'

'Petra, you know I didn't mean that. It's just that nearly every time I see you I seem to drag you into bed.'

'I certainly wasn't dragged. You must think I'm promiscuous.'

'Now, that is just silly. I think you are—'

She never knew. From outside came a tiny wail. She rolled off the bed, walked onto the patio and picked up her baby. For a while she rocked her. Then she came back inside, sat on the couch and put the baby to her breast.

Dominic was standing there, not knowing what to say or do, his face a mask of uncertainty.

For a while there was silence. Then the familiar calmness that came with breastfeeding stole over her.

'Having a new baby is a full-time job,' she told him. 'I'm not angry with you, I'm not even angry with myself for what we nearly got into. Thank you for dealing with Ken, he won't be a problem again. But now I've got enough on my plate without having to think about or worry about you. So I'd like you to go now.'

He looked at her uncertainly, and she realised that he didn't really know what to say or do. Just for once the dynamic Dominic Tate was at a loss. And he didn't like it.

Then he took a card from his pocket, scribbled something on it. 'That's my personal mobile phone number. Only half a dozen people have it. I want you to promise me that if anything at all causes you trouble, you'll call me.'

She reached and put the card on a shelf. 'All right,' she said.

He seemed distracted. 'The next few days are going to be horrendous,' he said. 'My consultant is away, I'll be doing most of his work as well as my own. I doubt if I'll have time to see you and—'

'Just do the next few days,' she told him. 'Take things one day at a time. And I'm not sure that I need to see you anyway.'

He stepped forward. Bent and kissed the top of Eleanor's tiny head. Then he kissed Petra on the cheek.

'You can call me at any time,' he said. 'I'm never parted from that mobile.' Then he left.

That was an eventful evening, Petra thought.

She was more tired than usual when she went to bed that night. It was her own fault. After Dominic had gone she had wandered round the flat tidying things, organising things, making lists of what she needed to do, what she needed to buy, reading through the vast amount of paperwork that seemed to come with having a baby.

Of course she knew what she was doing. She was trying to occupy her mind so she didn't have to think about what had just happened. Now she was in bed, the light off, the little sound of Eleanor's breathing echoing in her ears. Now she had to think.

What had happened between her and Dominic? Whose fault had it been, his or hers? Had she led him on in some way? And what could have happened?

A nursing mother wasn't usually considered the sexiest thing on earth. But she had tried to keep herself looking reasonably smart. Whether they could have made love was another matter. She was still sore from the operation. Perhaps not everything—but they could have made each other happy in some way or another. And with a growing dismay, she realised that she would have liked that.

What had happened between them? It hadn't been just sex, at least not on her part. And there was a limit to the extent she could blame her hormones. She had to admit it. She had wanted Dominic to kiss her, to— well, to go on. She had done it because... All she would allow herself to think was that she had some kind of regard for him. Not love. Definitely not love.

And then it struck her. It was Dominic who was falling in love. But he wasn't in love with her. He was in love with the baby.

She didn't think further about Dominic after that. She had her life to lead, her flat to run, her baby to look after. But slowly she was recovering. Her life was very comfortable. But she felt that sooner or later she would have to think about work. Only part time, of course. Eleanor would always come first. But she thought she needed something to occupy her mind. In a rare moment of self-knowledge she realised that she was thinking about work to stop herself thinking about Dominic.

Five days later, in the middle of the afternoon, there was the sound of her doorbell. She looked through her little spyhole first—after Ken she didn't want any more unpleasant surprises. Outside was a little girl, Petra guessed aged about eight. She was holding a small bunch of flowers. Her face was set, this was a determined and serious little girl. Petra opened the door.

'My name is Penelope Tate,' the little girl said. 'Could I see my cousin, please? This is the first one I've got. And I've brought these flowers for you, they're out of my garden.'

Petra took the flowers—another lovely bunch of summer roses—and blinked. She was unsure what to make of this. Penelope Tate? Wanting to see her cousin?

'Have you come here on your own?' she asked at last.

'No. Daddy's in the car outside. He said that if I wanted something badly, then I had to do something about it myself. And I wanted to see my cousin.'

'Eleanor? My daughter? Your cousin?'

'Yes. Uncle Dom told me I had a cousin. My daddy is his brother.'

'Let's go and see your daddy,' Petra said. 'Perhaps he'd like to see the baby, too.'

This was all new to her. She was an orphan, had no relations whatsoever. It came as a shock to her to realise that Eleanor might be different. Eleanor could have relations—through Dominic.

Petra stepped through the door and Penelope took her hand. 'This way,' she said, and led Petra down the path, turned towards the little car park. There was a car parked there, a man standing by it. As Petra drew nearer she knew it could only be Dominic's brother. They had a similar build, a similar face, the same coloured hair. But this man looked quieter, more ordinary. He didn't have the instant magnetic attraction that Dominic had.

He smiled as Petra approached him. 'I hope you'll forgive the intrusion,' he said, 'but since Penny here learned that there was a new member of the family, she's been on at us to come and visit. I'm Jack Tate, Dominic's younger brother. Is this a good time to call?'

Petra liked him at once, and took the outstretched hand. 'It's a perfect time to call,' she said. 'Come in. I'm just making some tea.'

She led them into her flat, straight to where Eleanor was lying in her pram, gently grizzling. Penny was obviously entranced. She peered into the pram. 'My cousin is very small,' she said.

'She was born just a bit too soon. But she'll grow in time. See if she'll hold your finger.'

Penny put a finger into Eleanor's palm, and turned amazed eyes to her father. 'She's holding onto me,' she said. 'She's gripping my finger.'

'Babies have strong grips,' said Petra. 'Now, would

you like to push the pram back and forwards a bit, see if you can get her to sleep? And I'll fetch you some orange juice.'

Penny was fascinated by her little job. Petra took Jack to sit in the living room and poured him a cup of tea. 'Dominic's never mentioned having a family,' she said. 'It's a bit of a shock.'

'I can imagine.' Jack looked a little uneasy. 'I should tell you that our coming here isn't Dom's idea, he doesn't know we've come round. If it's anyone's idea, it's Penny's. Dom told her first that she had a cousin. She wanted to come at once, he said that perhaps she could in a week or two. But Penny tends to be persistent so…here we are.'

'Dominic told you about me—about us?'

'Not a lot. He can be very secretive. After…well, he's changed since he was a boy. When we said we wanted to meet you, wanted to see the baby, he said that things were difficult but perhaps in time.'

'Difficult's a good word,' Petra said.

From behind them they heard a plaintive wail, and shortly afterwards a worried Penny came and said, 'I'm trying pushing her but she just won't got to sleep.'

'No. She needs bathing and feeding. Would you like to help?' Petra looked at Jack, her eyebrows raised.

Jack nodded. 'I've got a couple of boring errands in town,' he said. 'If I could leave Penny here for a while, that would be great.'

'Please, can I stay…? What do I call you?'

'Auntie Petra would be nice,' said Petra. She'd never been an auntie before.

'And are you and Uncle Dom going to—?'

'Penny!' Her father's voice was stern. 'I've told you not to ask personal questions!' He turned to Petra apologetically and said. 'Sorry, but…'

'It is difficult,' Petra agreed, 'but don't worry, we'll cope. You can leave me and Penny together now.'

'No more personal questions,' her father warned her, and then bent to kiss his slightly woebegone daughter.

Petra thought that was lovely.

Penny loved wearing an apron and washing the baby in the tiny bath. Then she sat and watched, fascinated, as Petra fed Eleanor. When her father returned she went to let him in, and Petra didn't mind that Jack could see her feeding. And Jack didn't seem at all awkward about it.

'So how will Dominic take it when he hears you've been to see us?' Petra asked quietly.

Jack shrugged. 'I think he'll be happy enough,' he said. 'But coming here was my decision—and Penny's decision. We all make up our own minds.'

'It's a family trait I've noticed,' Petra said drily.

With Penny's help, Eleanor was dressed and placed in her cot. Then Penny stayed to rock her and Jack and Petra talked quietly themselves.

But Jack didn't seem to know where to start. Petra thought he had something to say but didn't know how to say it. He started to speak half a dozen times, then broke off to ask some unrelated question about Petra's work. Eventually Petra smiled at him and said, 'Come

on, Jack, either tell me or don't. There's something
on your mind. I promise you, whatever it is, it won't
affect the way I see either you or Penny.'

'It might affect the way Dominic sees us,' muttered
Jack, 'but I suppose that's a chance I'll have to take.
And I really don't want to interfere. But…look, I'll
risk offending you first. Are you and Dom going to
get married—or even set up home together?'

'There's something about the Tate men, isn't
there?' Petra asked. 'They don't mind getting stuck
into a situation. They don't mind asking the difficult
questions.'

Jack shrugged. 'I only asked because I want my
brother to be happy. And now I've met you, I very
much want you to be happy too.'

'Well, I'll just say that we have no plans to get
together at the moment. In fact, at times I'm not too
sure I like him that much.'

'He can be an awkward so and so.'

He was silent for a moment. Then he stood and
went into the bedroom, looked at his daughter rocking
Eleanor. When he came back he seemed to have made
up his mind.

'I'm going to stick my neck out and tell you something that I think you ought to know. It's not my
secret—in fact, it isn't a secret, a lot of people know
about it. And you should. You might not like it, but
you should know.'

By now Petra was fascinated. 'Go on,' she said. 'I
promise I'll be…I'll not be judgmental or anything.
Well, I'll try not to be.'

'Being judgmental is not what I'm afraid of.

Now…' He sat upright on the couch, fixed his eyes on the opposite side of the room. 'About five years ago Dom was a lot easier to live with than he is now. Though he was still a lot more excitable than me. He was going out with a girl called Alice Myers, they were pretty serious. She was a bit younger than him, a junior doctor. We all liked her, got on with her— but she was too much like Dominic. She was too quick to jump to conclusions, she found it too easy to lose her temper. Perhaps in time she would have calmed down.'

'Not the ideal partner for Dominic.'

'You're telling me. But they really loved each other. And then Alice fell pregnant. It was a planned baby.'

'One of those,' Petra muttered, then felt a bit guilty. Whatever it was, this wasn't Jack's fault. 'Sorry, go on,' she said.

'Well, they had decided not to get married—much to my mother's irritation. But things were going fine. Alice had had a scan and they knew that the baby would be a little girl. Then one evening they had a really big row. Dominic said it was all about nothing really. Alice walked out in a temper.'

Petra could tell that Jack wasn't liking this bit. His face was pale and he kept licking his lips.

'Alice had a little orange sports car. Perhaps she drove too fast, we don't know. Perhaps there were other cars on the road, that stretch between here and Calthorpe attracts too many drunks. Anyway, she crashed, rolled off the road. They got her into A and E barely alive. Fortunately Dominic wasn't on duty. She died of her injuries after a few minutes. The baby was delivered, for a while she was viable. But then she died, too. And it changed Dominic completely.'

'Did he blame himself?'

'Possibly. He's never been the same since.' Jack swallowed. 'Since then he's never been in a relationship with a woman that's lasted more than three months. He told me that looking for something long-lasting just wasn't worth the effort.'

Petra was silent for a while. Then she said, 'The baby that died. They were going to call her Charlotte, weren't they?'

Jack looked at her, surprised. 'How did you know that?'

'Just a hint he once dropped,' Petra said.

Penny came into the room then and said that Eleanor was asleep. Was there anything else she could do to help?

'We don't want to overtire Auntie Petra,' Jack said. 'We'd better go now, but perhaps you can come back again some time.'

'We can take the baby for a walk in the park,' said Petra. 'You can push the pram. Jack, I'm so glad you called. You've given me such a lot to think about.'

His smile was gentle. 'He's an awkward one, isn't he? Hope to see more of you quite soon, Petra.'

Petra sat on her couch, having seen them out, took a deep breath and breathed out with a sigh. It had been an enjoyable afternoon, she had really liked Penny and Jack. But in a way she was now glad that they'd gone. She had so much to think about. Things that had upset her before now made sense.

First there was a sadness, overlaid by the prospect of pleasure to come. She had never really had a family of her own. She had so much liked the couple of Dominic's family that she had just met and she suspected that she would like the rest too when she met them.

She would have liked a family of her own. She had friends, of course, but now could guess at the special comfort and support that a family could bring. She knew that Eleanor would benefit from having a cousin like Penny, an uncle like Jack. But that was only half a family. What she needed was a father.

With a little shiver of apprehension, Petra realised that this might not be a problem. She thought that Dominic would be a good father—if she let him. Mother love was something that was often immediate, father love tended to grow more slowly. She had seen it grow often enough in the unit, after the first fright of seeing a child so small. And Dominic was showing all the signs of growing to be a loving father.

Already she had seen the way his eyes turned to his child. In her mind now there was no doubt. Dominic would grow to love Eleanor. This left one thing. What did Dominic feel about *her?*

Petra knew that there could be a great, wonderful physical passion between them. That was splendid but it wasn't enough. Passion was great but she needed love.

Now that Jack had explained to her about Alice Myers, she felt that she understood Dominic much,

much better. The story of the death of his girlfriend and his child had chilled her. And she knew that the apparently toughest men often felt things the most. They had no way of letting their emotions show. But life had to move on. It was time for Dominic to come into the present, not remain fixated on the past.

So where did this leave her? All right, Admit it to herself. She could…easily…fall in love with Dominic. She didn't love him yet. Not quite. That was, she didn't think she loved him yet. She had a baby to consider, she couldn't love him! Not until he showed some feeling for her.

CHAPTER SIX

PETRA drew up outside number 25 Thornton Avenue. It was a pleasant double-fronted house in a tree-lined suburb on the outskirts of Denham. She reached into the back of the car, started to unstrap Eleanor's carrycot. In the boot was the pram chassis, the cot would fit straight into it.

Penny ran down the drive to help her, obviously she had been watching. 'Can I push her into the house?' she asked. 'In fact, round the back of the house. We're all sitting out there 'cos it's warm.'

'Sounds a good idea,' Petra said.

She wasn't really sure about this, was feeling a bit uneasy. Jack had phoned her and had invited her and Eleanor to tea. Petra was to meet Mary, his wife, and Sally, his mother. Who was, of course, Dominic's mother.

She felt as if she was acquiring a set of in-laws without a husband. It seemed to be doing things the wrong way round. Still, she had accepted.

With Penny in front, pushing the pram, they went round the side of the house. There was a canopy erected on the lawn and a set of garden chairs round a central table. Everyone stood as Penny shouted, 'Look who's come.' Petra walked forward.

First Jack introduced her to Mary, a smiling woman who kissed Petra and said she'd heard so much about her. Then there was Sally. She was tall, had silver hair and in spite of the fact that she must be at least in her mid-fifties, looked ten years younger. She too kissed Petra, and hugged her. 'It's so good to meet you,' she said. And there was sincerity in her voice. Petra wondered why Sally was so pleased to see her.

'And this is Eleanor,' Petra said. Everyone peered in the pram, and Eleanor, presumably realising she was the centre of attention, opened her eyes and gurgled.

'If you put your finger in her hand, she'll squeeze it,' said Penny. So Sally and Mary put their fingers into Eleanor's hand.

'Why don't we all stay out here and have a cool drink?' Jack said. 'And if you don't mind, Penny will push Eleanor round the garden.'

'Eleanor would like that,' said Petra. So they sat under the canopy and enjoyed a glass of iced homemade lemonade.

For a while the conversation was general. Then Jack and Mary disappeared into the house to prepare tea and Petra was left alone with Sally. She felt just a little apprehensive. There was too much of Dominic's toughness in Sally's eyes. Petra suspected that she could be a formidable lady.

'This is difficult,' said Sally, though not showing many signs of any difficulty. 'I had hoped that when I was shown my second grandchild both mother and father would be present. Seems reasonable. But I want you to know, Petra, that whatever happens between you and my errant son, we want to see you and Eleanor for yourselves. I don't want to talk about you and him, that's your problem. You sort it out in your own way, I suspect you've got the character for it. Just remember there's always a place here, or in my home, for you and your baby.'

'That's a lovely thing to say,' Petra faltered. 'Apart from anything else, I think Eleanor would love a grandmother. And I can't give her one.'

'That's settled, then. Now, I gather you are a nurse. I was a nurse myself not too many years ago. Tell me about working in SCBU.'

'I love it. And now I've had my own baby looked after there, I know just how important the work is. Well, I knew before, but now I can feel it. And it makes a difference.'

'I'm sure it does. Are you thinking of going back?'

'Not straight away, but eventually. And only for a few hours a week. In a few months, once I've got Eleanor settled, I'll think about it. I don't need the money, I need the...' She realised that she was about to say something that might be taken the wrong way.

But Sally knew what she meant. 'You need the companionship, and since you don't have a live-in partner, you want to get it at work. Very understandable. Is there a crèche at the hospital?'

'There is. But not for very young babies. Finding somewhere where I'd be happy leaving Eleanor is going to be difficult.'

'Have you heard of the Sandpit?'

Petra had heard of it. It was a small and exclusive crèche. A lot of the senior hospital staff left their babies there and were very happy with it. 'I've heard of it. But I gather there's a very long waiting list.

They say you put your baby's name down for the Sandpit before it's even conceived.'

'That's good to know. Petra, I own the Sandpit. I'm the manager and sole proprietor. When you think you're ready, why don't you come and look round? See if you think Eleanor would be happy there. And I'm always on the lookout for good staff. You could work with me there and do some time at SCBU.'

Petra's head was buzzing. 'This is all too much,' she muttered. 'It just can't go on. Suddenly it seems as if everything's going my way. I'd love to come and work with you at the Sandpit when Eleanor's older. I can't think of a better way of easing back into working life. You're being so good to me and...'

To her horror she found tears trickling down her cheeks. She seemed to have wept more in the past few weeks than ever before in her life. And she should be happy!

Casually, Sally passed her a tissue. 'Still hormonal,' she said with a grin. 'After I had Dominic I wept every day for a year. And it irritated me! Don't worry, you do get over it. Now, do I hear the rattle of teacups?'

I think I'll get Eleanor out to join the party,' said Petra.

She felt she was in the family. She sat and fed her baby while tea was laid on the table in front of her. And then they ate, and everyone held Eleanor for a while. Penny held her most carefully, sitting next to Petra and terrified of doing something wrong. Sally held her with obvious confidence. But there was something in the way that she looked at the baby that

made Petra certain that she'd be a doting grandmother. Petra felt that she'd been parachuted into a
ready-made family. And she loved it.

They talked about odd things—about Jack's work
as a solicitor, and about Mary's part-time job as an
infant teacher. At times it was difficult. Dominic's
name seemed to come up in the conversation and it
was a little embarrassing to have to avoid talking
about him. But they managed. Petra noticed that not
once did Penny refer to her Uncle Dom, and suspected that she had been told not to. Well, that was
thoughtful.

Eventually it was time to go. Petra insisted that
they all come to her flat for tea the following week.
'We'd love to come to see where you live,' said
Mary. 'But on one condition. We bring the food.
You've got enough to do looking after that baby.'

And this Petra had to accept.

Petra had thoroughly enjoyed her afternoon and
was looking forward to seeing her newfound family
again. Perhaps because if this, she felt a bit lonely
that night. Her flat was wonderful, but it was still a
home only to herself and her baby. She needed...she
needed a man there. No, it was more than that, she
needed Dominic there.

She realised she was thinking of him more and
more. Her body was recovering from the effects of
having a baby by Caesarean section. She found herself remembering more and more often just what their
one night of passion had been like. She went though
each detail, each recollected feeling until she felt quite
uncomfortable. She needed him.

This is just your body reacting, an internal voice suggested. You don't need Dominic Tate—you need any man. But she knew that wasn't true. She needed more than Dominic's body, she wanted to possess all of him. Love wasn't a word to bandy around. She wouldn't let herself think about love. But Dominic could be a lovable man. Pity he didn't love her. Far, far too late, she went to sleep.

She woke next morning thinking about Dominic and after feeding and bathing her baby she was still thinking of him. 'That man's getting to be a pain,' she told Eleanor. 'He's getting into my mind where he has no business to be. I've got other things to be thinking about.'

Eleanor gurgled and blew a big bubble. 'Exactly,' said Petra.

At midmorning her phone rang. Good, friends often rang at this time for a quick chat. Someone to take her mind off Dominic.

'Is that the family member Petra?' a voice asked.

It was Dominic! The last person she had expected to hear from! And because it was unexpected she blurted out, 'I was just thinking of you.'

'That's very nice. Good things, I hope. Sorry not to have been in touch before, but things here have been fraught. I gather you've met my family?'

His voice was calm, collected, she couldn't tell what his reaction was. 'Yes, I have, and I like them all very much. Are you angry with me?'

He sounded amused. 'Certainly not. Why should I be? Anyway, we all make our own minds up, we're an independent family that way. And I'm very fond of Penny, she's the most independent of us all. Now, how's Eleanor?'

'Your daughter is fine.'

'You said that deliberately, as if making fun of me. I know she's my daughter, I've never denied it.'

Petra laughed. 'You're coming to love her, aren't you? She's no longer something appallingly unexpected or a responsibility that you have to take on. She's a person, your child, half of you, and you're coming to love her.'

There was a long silence. Then he said, 'I think things are getting out of hand between you and me, Petra. I've got the day after tomorrow free. Could I take you and Eleanor out for the day? We could enjoy ourselves and perhaps have a talk.'

'All right. I think I'd like that. Get here about ten. Or earlier and you watch me bath her. Or you could bath her yourself.'

There was another silence. 'I will come early,' he said. 'And, Petra—'

'We'll talk when you come. Looking forward to it, Dominic.' And she rang off.

She now felt less alone than she had before. But she felt more confused. What did she want from Dominic? What was he offering her? She didn't know.

Losing himself in work had always been easy for Dominic. There was the usual mixture of cases in A and E, some serious, some trivial, some of which had no business being in the department at all. But he dealt with them all. And he enjoyed himself.

When he had finished work he picked up his kit and went to the hospital courts to play squash. It was a hard, demanding game and his opponent was as good as himself. After an hour he was panting, bathed in sweat, and could feel his heart beating like a giant drum. He had needed to push himself. But after showering and returning to his flat for a scratch meal, he still felt restless. He wanted something. He didn't know what. For a moment he considered phoning Melanie and asking her if she fancied a drink. Then he decided against it. He hadn't been in touch with her for days. And he didn't want to take her for a drink.

Instead he walked to the local pub himself. It would be full of hospital staff, perhaps there'd be someone there he could enjoy talking to. And there was Susie, laughing with a crowd of younger nurses.

She noticed him come in, and when he didn't walk over to them came over to speak to him. 'Not joining us, Dom? You're very welcome.'

'I'd be bad company, Susie. I don't feel I'm in the mood for mixing with happy, cheerful people.'

'You do sound gloomy. Tell you what, you buy me a drink and take it into the back room. I'll join you there in a minute. This is a hen night—Eunice there is getting married at the weekend. And the gang wants to move on to the Cross Foxes, they've got a band there. But I'm not as young as them. And I hate pubs with music!'

She joined him five minutes later. 'What's the trouble, then? Something wrong with the joys of father-hood?'

He winced. One of Susie's strengths as a nurse was that she would take no nonsense from a patient. She would ask a question and expect it to be answered.

'Well, I've just learned that my family have been touch with Petra. She's been to my brother's for tea, met my mother and the rest of the family. Apparently they're all getting on very well. I can't sort out what's happening, I feel boxed in. People are taking decisions about my life that I ought to be taking myself.'

Susie laughed. 'You're feeling left out,' she said. 'Remember, there's not just you, there's Petra, Eleanor, your mother, Penny and your brother and his wife. They've all got feelings, they're all entitled to do what they want about them.'

'Even go to see the baby?'

'Especially go to see the baby. Your baby. In fact, I want to see her myself.'

'Very helpful,' he snarled, drinking his beer. 'Any-way, I'm taking Petra and the baby out for a day the day after tomorrow. Perhaps we can get things sorted. Do you know a walk we can do where it's possible to push a pram?'

'I'll put a map of one on your desk tomorrow morning.' Susie waited a moment and then gently asked, 'You're all mixed up aren't you? And you don't like it.'

'I certainly don't like it. And I am mixed up. I think I know what I feel for Eleanor. It's the kind of love I never expected to feel. And I know what I feel for

Petra and Eleanor together. There's love there too. But I've got to separate out what I feel for Petra, without any other considerations.'

'Being the mother of your child is a pretty big consideration,' Susie said mildly, 'but I do know what you mean. Anyway, from what you tell me, Petra is a real catch. You should ask her to marry you.'

'Ask her to marry me! I'm not ready. I just can't think about it.'

'You are in a mess,' said Susie. 'Come here and give me a hug.'

So he hugged her. And he wondered just how valuable her advice was.

Simon! Come in, it's good to see you.'

'It's good to see you too, Petra. You're looking well.' He looked at her irresolutely, so she put her arms round him and kissed him. Just a friendly kiss, of course. But then he smiled.

'I've brought these flowers for you…and here's a dress for Eleanor. One of the nurses knitted it for me, you must tell me if it's the right—'

'It's lovely. Now stop talking and come in.'

It was the same night. Simon had phoned earlier, saying he was in Denham just for the night and would it be convenient for him to call? Of course it was. He had rung her quite regularly from London, telling her about his course and asking after her and Eleanor.

After she had learned about the money she had won she could tell that he had been a little unsure of things. She had had to insist that the money meant less to her than friends. And he would always be one of her friends.

He looked at Eleanor, asked technical medical questions about her and seemed very happy with the answers. He said he'd like a cup of tea but that there was no need whatsoever for her to make him a sandwich. He looked uncomfortable.

And slowly she realised what it was. Dominic had been right. Simon was in love with her. Not just the infatuation or regard that she had really always known about, but properly in love. And now he just didn't know what to say, where to go. She had started a new life without him, and he suspected that he would never be a part of it. She felt sad for him.

'Do you see much of Dr Tate?' he carefully asked. 'Have there been any developments there?'

'There's nothing settled. But he is Eleanor's father and he comes over to see her from time to time.'

'To see her or to see you?'

She had to give an honest answer, even if it was a cruel one. 'I don't really know. Perhaps a bit of both. We're getting on better now. I'm not as angry as I was before.'

'I see,' said Simon, though it was obvious that he didn't.

'Whatever it is, you'll always be my friend, and the person who managed to get the blood that saved the life of my daughter. If she had been a boy I would have called him Simon.'

He smiled. 'That's one of the nicest things anyone has ever said to me,' he said.

He didn't stay too long—said he didn't want to

overtire her. She thought that was an excuse. And when he'd gone she felt rather sad again. In many ways he would have made a wonderful husband. He'd be kind, thoughtful, a good father. If she could just fall for him—but she couldn't. Simon would never make her pulses race the way that Dominic did. It was just too bad.

She was looking forward to her day out with Dominic. She was also curious, they had never been out together for pleasure before. Apart from their first frenzied meeting, that was. Every time they met they had problems to solve, things to discuss. Probably they'd discuss things this time. But there should be some pleasure too.

She woke early. The forecast was good, the sun already warm. She had prepared a bag of everything she might need for Eleanor and was wondering what to wear herself. Her figure was now nearly back to the lissom shape it had been before Eleanor had been conceived, she was rather proud of that. So she decided to show it off a little. Light blue chinos—she had admired the ones Dominic wore and had bought a pair deliberately. And a darker blue T-shirt. Under it she was still wearing her nursing bra, not the garment to make the very most of her figure. But, she thought as she appraised herself in the mirror, she didn't look too bad.

The doorbell rang, and there he was on the step. He was dressed similarly to her, but in drill chinos and a dark red T-shirt. She had been expecting him but still her heart thumped when she opened the door. And he looked gorgeous.

He also looked rather strained, as if he wasn't sure what he was doing there. Well, neither was she. But she wasn't going to show it.

'Well, I'm ready to go,' she said, 'but there's a little girl in her chair who is not ready. She'd been fed, but do you want to change her and bath her?'

'If that's meant to be a challenge, it's unsuccessful,' he said. 'I've changed and bathed enough infants in my time to be reasonably proficient. Lead me to it. I can do more than cope, I can do well.'

So she pointed to the changing mat and the pile of clothes, led him to the bathroom. 'She's all yours,' Petra said.

And then she had a shock, when he replied, 'All mine?'

For a moment she watched, but he was obviously as proficient as he had said. So she went to make him a drink, and listened to the gurgles of delight coming from the bathroom. The two of them seemed to be having a fine time and momentarily she felt left out. He'll have to know that we're a team, she thought to herself. Petra and Eleanor. We come together.

Eventually they were ready. He dressed Eleanor very competently in the clothes that Petra had put out, and then they went out to his car. It took two journeys to carry all the things that would be, or could be, necessary. 'Do all babies need this amount of baggage?' he asked.

'Think yourself lucky. I've cut things down to the bare essentials. Where are we going?'

'Susie gave me a map of a walk high on the moors.
It's shaded and it's negotiable by pram. I think you'll
enjoy it.'

'Looking forward to it already,' she said.

It was now very warm out but his car had air-
conditioning. She was able to select the exact temperature to suit Eleanor. It must be nice to have
enough money to buy a car with air-conditioning, she
thought. Then she remembered. She had enough
money.

They said little while he drove. But after half an
hour he parked in a picnic spot and helped her get
out the pram. 'Apparently we can walk along the
ridge,' he said. 'There's a good path and the views
over the Vale are terrific.'

'So let's go.'

'Shall I push the pram?'

For a moment she was reluctant to let him. Eleanor
was *her* baby. But then she thought that was silly. Of
course he could push the pram.

It was a good walk, and strangely quiet. Perhaps
people were moving on towards the sea. For a while
they walked in silence, enjoying the tranquillity,
smelling the turpentine smell of the pine trees and the
distant hint of sea salt. He pushed the pram and she
wondered if she should take his arm. Then she
thought it would look awkward.

'How did you get on with my family?' he asked
after a while.

'I liked them very much. They are kind and
thoughtful and they seem determined to love
Eleanor.'

'If you like them then you should like me. We are similar.'

'There are differences,' she said. 'Have you talked to them about me?'

'Only in the very broadest terms. They know that I am Eleanor's father. They know that there was not...a lot between us before she was born.'

'About five hours,' Petra muttered. 'So there's been no family conference. No joint decision about what to do about me?'

'No. And there won't be. If I want advice, I'll ask for it. If I don't want it, it won't be offered.'

'Now there's the Dominic I recognise,' said Petra. 'Don't you ever get tired of having the answer to everything?'

'I wish I did have the answer. I don't know what to do about you, for a start.'

'You don't have to do anything,' Petra said tartly. 'At the moment I can look after myself and after Eleanor. We're independent. We select our own friends. We don't actually need you.'

She turned to look at him, and could tell by the scowl on his face that this wasn't the news that he wanted to hear. So she added, 'But we're both enjoying your company this morning. Aren't we, Eleanor?'

Perhaps wisely, Eleanor didn't comment.

'I know what my mother wants,' he said after a couple of minutes. 'She won't tell me unless I ask her, but I already know what she wants.'

'And that is?'

'She'd like me married.'

It was the first time the word had been mentioned

between them. It seemed to separate them as they both considered it. Then, carefully, she said, 'You marry someone when you love them, when you think you can make them happy and you want to spend the rest of your life with them.'

'Sounds a good plan,' he agreed.

'Whereas you think you have been pushed towards me. Through no fault of yours, fate has conspired to make me the woman you ought to marry. Whether you want to or not.'

Again there was a silence. 'I feel I ought...' he started. 'But then the last thing you should do is get married because you feel you ought... I think I like you a lot, Petra, but I'm not sure if I...if I...'

'The word you're looking for is "love," she said. 'And if you can't even say it, I'm sure you can't feel it. I think that wraps things up between us.'

He stared bleakly into the far distance. 'I'm scared,' he said. 'I don't want to make a mistake— for your sake and for Eleanor's sake as well as my own.'

She could only guess at what it had cost him to make that confession. She put her hand on the pram handle, stopped him pushing it. Then she turned him towards her, reached out and hugged him. Then, quickly, she released him. 'I'll bet it hurt you to say that,' she said, 'and I appreciate it. But there's something else you haven't considered.'

'And that is?'

'How do I feel about you? Love is a two-way process, Dominic. You both take and give. I'm not sure what I feel for you. After all, I've not seen much of you.'

'That,' he said carefully, 'is true.'

'We'll help you, Eleanor and me, we'll get to know you and we'll help you get to know us. But there's something you should know. I'm not going to hang about all my life waiting for you to make up your mind. I need a life, too. Eleanor and I need a life, and we're going to have one.'

'That's fair enough.' He turned to smile at her and it was as if the sun had suddenly come out. 'Look, that's enough deep thoughts for a lovely day like this. Let's just enjoy ourselves. And perhaps some kind of salvation for us will sneak up when we're not looking for it.'

'Always a possibility,' she said.

For the rest of the walk they were happy to walk side by side in contented silence. Then they got back to the car and he said, 'Now for the next bit of excitement. I've got somewhere else in mind to take you.'

This time they drove down towards the coast. After a while he turned off the main road and carefully negotiated a bumpy little unpaved road that led through fields and past small woods. Every now and again there was a glimpse of the sea, sparkling and blue ahead of them. She thought she had been here years before, but it was not a well-known place.

They parked by the cliff edge. Below them was a small cove, with a path winding down to it. Dominic carried Eleanor down in her carrycot while Petra followed, carrying the bag of baby necessities. They found somewhere to sit, in the shade of a giant rock, and as she made herself comfortable on a blanket, he went back to the car for the picnic basket. He had told her that he would see to all the food—she was just to enjoy the day.

There was no one else on the beach so she felt more than happy to sit there and feed the baby. Then he scrambled back down and sat by her side. He brought a basket and a big white container.

'What's in the plastic container?'

'Just fresh water. I thought...I wondered...if it was really warm I might take my daughter for her first-ever salt-water swim. Then we could wash the salt off her afterwards.'

'The sea will be far too cold!'

He pointed to where, a few yards away, there was a pool in the rocks. 'That water will have been warmed by the sun. She could splash in there for a couple of minutes.'

Petra thought for a moment. 'All right,' she said. 'You know she loves being bathed. But if she yells, she's straight out.'

'I'll test the water first. With my elbow.'

'And are you going to get in dressed like that?'

'I'll change,' he said. 'I've brought a couple of towels and my shorts.'

She rather liked the casual way in which he changed by her side. And she liked looking at his body even more. He was tall, muscular, and his body excited her. But, then, it always had.

She took off the few clothes that Eleanor was wearing and he carried her to the rock pool. Then he lay in the pool full length and let the baby rest on his chest. She squealed with delight when he gently dropped handfuls of water on her. 'She's going to be a water-baby,' he said.

He didn't keep her there long. After a while he brought her out. Petra dampened a cloth with the fresh water and washed off the salt. 'She's going to sleep now,' she said.

'You can bet on it. Now, give me five minutes, I feel the need for exercise.'

He ran to the water's edge, waded out a few feet and then threw himself into the waves. She might have guessed that he'd be a good swimmer. He did a rapid crawl out to sea—so far that she worried just a little—then turned and made an equally speedy return. He ran up the beach towards her and she passed him the cloth she had used to wipe off Eleanor. 'Here. Rub yourself down with this or you'll feel sticky.'

So he did. Then he lay by her side with his back against the rock and reached out his arms for the baby. Petra passed her to him. And he held his child against his bare chest until the baby slept.

'It's a nice feeling, isn't it?' she asked him after a while. 'Having her skin so close to yours?'

'Yes, it's a nice feeling. Sometimes I wonder what it would be like to be a woman. To be so close to your baby.'

'Don't wonder,' she advised him. 'It's hard work. And as for having babies…'

He held up just one arm. 'All right, I give in. But this is nice.'

She saw the way he glanced down at the now sleeping Eleanor. It was a look of fascination, of love. She knew the feeling, the wonder that you were the parent of something as small but as perfect as this. But then he looked at her and his expression was much more guarded. She wondered what he wanted from her.

'This baby is now asleep,' he said, 'and the cold water has made me hungry. How about you?'

She took Eleanor from him, arranged her in her carrycot and made sure both that she was covered and that she was not in the sun. 'I guess I'm hungry too,' she said. 'What have you got in the magic basket?'

'You'll be surprised.'

First he spread a cloth. Then he took out plates, glasses and cutlery. Finally there was a bewildering array of plastic containers. From somewhere he produced a salad bowl and proceeded to fill it with salad and then drip on a dressing.

'Did you prepare all this?' she asked faintly.

'Some of it. I borrowed the basket from Susie, and she told me what to buy and where to go.'

There was a bottle of white wine in a chilled container. There were rolls in a cloth, a variety of meats, three different salads. To finish there were washed cherries and strawberries with a carton of cream. It was a feast. And when they had finished there was coffee from a Thermos.

'That was the best meal I've had in months,' she said. 'It was truly wonderful.'

'Wonderful because of the company.' He leaned over to inspect the sleeping Eleanor.

'You can babysit for a while. I haven't brought my swimming costume but I can take off my chinos and go for a paddle. There's no one around to see me in my knickers.'

'I can see you in your knickers,' he said placidly, 'and I like it.'

So she went for a paddle. And as the small waves broke gently against her knees she looked back up the beach, at him, at Eleanor. He was repacking the basket, keeping a careful eye on his daughter. She thought that they must look like an ideal couple. Two people together on the beach, with their child.

But they weren't a couple. After a while her legs began to feel cold. The afternoon was passing.

She walked back up the beach to him, accepted the cloth to wash down her legs and said, 'I don't think we ought to stay out too long. We might overtire the baby quite without intending to. She's had a lovely day, but it's time she was back in her own home, her own room.'

He rolled easily to his feet. 'Whatever you say, you're both her mother and her nurse. But it's been lovely here. Do you think we can come back some time?'

'Possibly,' she said. Then she thought she was being a bit unfair to him so she said, 'Why don't you come back to my flat for tea? It won't be anything like what we've just had but I can manage toasted cheese sandwiches or eggs of some kind.'

'That would be great. And I can help put the baby to bed.'

Put the *baby* to bed? she thought.

Time seemed to be passing. It took longer than they had anticipated to get back to Denham, the holidaymakers were out in force. Once home she decided to bath Eleanor again—she wasn't too sure how well she had been rinsed after being in the sea. And while Dominic leaned over the bath and sprinkled water on his gurgling child, she made him the toasted cheese sandwiches she had promised him.

'Use anything out of the basket that's left over,' he shouted. 'It'll be no use to me.' So there would be toasted cheese sandwiches with extra meat and salads.

She fed Eleanor and put her down in her cot. Eleanor was tired and slept at once, and for a while Petra was anxious that she had done too much with the child. But all the signs were good. If Eleanor had been in an incubator in her ward, Petra would have been more than happy with her.

Next she and Dominic ate. There was half a bottle of the white wine left, he insisted that they finish it. Then she cleared away the dishes. When he offered to wash up she told him that things could wait.

To her surprise she saw that it was now getting dark. 'It's been a long day,' she muttered. 'Where has all the time gone?'

'It's gone quickly because we've been happy,' he said.

As he spoke she saw him rubbing the inside of his T-shirt. 'Don't tell me, you're itching,' she said.

'It's nothing. Probably I just didn't manage to rinse off all of the salt. I need a shower, I'll get one as soon as I'm back.'

'You can have one here if you want. Have one now.'

'All right,' he said after a pause. 'I'd like that.'

So he went for a shower and she wondered about what would happen next. What did she want to happen next? She was mistress of her own destiny.

She heard the thrumming of the shower and when it finished she had almost made up her mind. She knocked on the bathroom door. 'Towels in the big cupboard. May I come in?'

There was a pause and then she heard his muffled voice, 'I didn't lock the door. I thought it might be seen as unfriendly.'

For a moment she was poised, one hand on the doorknob, not yet knowing whether she was going to turn it or not. This was to be entirely her decision. Then she turned it and entered.

He was standing, looking at her, a grave, a thoughtful expression on his face. All he was wearing was a white towel, wrapped round him like a sarong. Once again she saw the muscled upper body, the trim waist. His longish hair was still wet, she could see drops of water falling onto his shoulders. There was a hunger in his eyes and that finally convinced her.

'It's not only men that have desires and feelings,' she told him, 'women do too. And I want you to come to bed with me. This is not a declaration of love or anything like that. It's just something that we both want and we do well together.'

'Are you sure?' he asked. But now she could see the flame of desire in his eyes.

'Yes, I'm quite sure. I know I'm a bit confused but I know what I want and what I need.' She bowed her head and then said, 'And I've missed you.'

'I've missed you too,' he said hoarsely.

She took his hand, led him into her bedroom. 'You lie here, wait for me. I want a shower too, it's been a warm day. And I'll come to you soon.'

Then she showered. From a drawer in the bathroom she took a nightie, then put it back. He must take her as she was. She dried herself and walked naked into the bedroom.

It was nearly dusk now, just the odd ray of the dying sun shone through her curtains. He had left off the light in the bedroom, his body was part light, part shadow. There was only a sheet on her bed, he was sitting upright with it pulled up to his waist.

She stood by the bed, picking a place so that her body was illuminated by the rosy glow of the sun. She slid her hand across the scar from her Caesarean section, making sure he could see it. 'You take me as I am,' she said, 'scar and all.'

'I can't see the scar,' he said. 'If I can it means nothing to me and it must mean nothing to you. I see you as simply beautiful. As you were before. Will you come to bed?'

She lifted the sheet, slid in beside him. 'Simple practicalities,' she said, 'though being a doctor I'm sure that you know. I've just had a slit cut in my lower abdomen. There's not a lot I can do. There were fireworks the last time we were together, there can be nothing like that tonight.'

'I'd be happy just to lie here with you,' he said. 'Just to hold you, to stroke you, to sleep with you. I can feel the warmth of your body, smell that scent that is only you. For me that will be plenty.'

To her surprise she found that she believed him. It

showed a depth of feeling, a delicacy that she hadn't known he possessed. But... 'I think we can do better than just lying together,' she said. 'Now, will you stop talking and kiss me?'

So he kissed her. And then, as the sun slowly set outside, they explored each other's body. They found a joy in touching and giving, found a pleasure in the gentlest of caresses that could speedily mount to an ecstasy she had previously only dreamed of.

'You're so good to me,' she panted. 'You make me so happy.'

'If you are happy then I am happy too.' And finally, bathed in the soft warmth of culmination, she slept. But before she did, a tiny corner of her mind noticed something. He hadn't said that he loved her. It would have been nice if he had.

CHAPTER SEVEN

SHE lived alone with her baby so Petra was a light sleeper. She woke as Dominic did early next morning, reached out a hand to him as he tried to slide quietly out of bed. He took her hand and kissed it. 'I have to go,' he whispered. 'I'm due at work and I can't be late. But you stay in bed, try to sleep, you need your rest. I'll be in touch.'

She didn't sleep at once. She heard him as, with the lightest of steps, he tiptoed over to look at the baby. There was a pause and then he moved away. Five minutes later she heard the front door click. And he was gone.

She stayed in bed until a small wail from Eleanor told her that it was time to feed her. Then she got out of bed, performed the customary early-morning ritual of feeding and bathing. Usually it was something that calmed her, pleased her. But this morning things were a bit different.

Eleanor was more grizzly than she had ever been. Petra didn't think there was anything seriously wrong with her, she was just having one of those tiny tantrums that all babies had at some time. But then she wondered if she and Dominic had overtired their child. Perhaps the day out had been a bit too much for her. She had seemed happy with everything—but she still wasn't very strong.

Petra wondered if she had been rather selfish, wanting to go out with Dominic instead of staying at home with her baby. Then she decided that this was not so. Eleanor had enjoyed herself. And after a while, after being rocked in her pram, Eleanor slept and was wheeled to her place on the patio. Now Petra had time to bath herself, to dress herself and make some breakfast. Then she had time to think. Why was she feeling vaguely dispirited?

Yesterday had been wonderful, last night had been blissful. It had been more blissful because she had initiated it. She had taken the decision, had made up her own mind. She was becoming more self-confident.

And they went so well together! It was as if each knew what the other wanted and needed, each knew how to give and take maximum pleasure. At times she had thought their two bodies had been one, their pleasure a doubled one.

But…he had not said he loved her. She knew he had had to leave early this morning, knew that he had had very little time. But he could have hinted that they had a future together. Did they have a future together?

She remembered Ken—no, there was no comparison! Ken was lead while Dominic was gold. But there was one thing she had to consider. She had stayed with Ken even though she had known it had been foolish. She should have cut her losses with him, left him months before she actually had. She had known there was no good future for her with Ken.

So how long should she wait, hoping that Dominic

would make some kind of commitment to her? To her, not to her—and his—baby? Yesterday she had warned him. When would it be time to think not of him but just of herself and her baby?

She smiled ironically to herself. What a time to discover that she was tough after all.

At lunchtime Simon phoned and sounded on top of the world. She tried desperately to sound equally cheerful for him but it was an effort and he saw through it. 'Have you got problems, Petra?'

'None that you don't know about. I'm an unmarried mother and it's not a state that I'm either happy or pleased about.' Then she laughed. 'Hear me complaining? How many unmarried mothers have had the good luck that I have?'

'You've got friends as well as luck,' Simon said. 'Look, I've got things to do, people to see about the hospital this afternoon. But may I come and see you later? I've had some news—good news—and you're the one I want to share it with.'

'Of course you can come round. You can come round any time. What kind of good news?'

'Tell you when I see you.' And he rang off, leaving her feeling both curious and pleased. She was glad Simon was happy. She was glad one of her friends could get it right.

When he arrived she could tell how full he was of his good fortune, but he wouldn't talk about it at once. 'You come first,' he said. 'This morning I could tell that you were down, and you can't fool me now.

Something has upset you. Tell me, it helps to share problems.'

So she told him just the bare outlines of the situation. 'It's Dominic. He comes here to see the baby, he dotes on her. But I don't know what his attitude to me is, and I'm not happy at having to hang around waiting to find out. Now, that's all I'm going to say on the subject. What's your news?'

Simon frowned. 'You might not know what Dominic's attitude to you is. Possibly he doesn't know himself. He might still be in shock.'

'He's had a few weeks to get over his shock,' Petra said. 'But it's generous-minded of you to say that. Now, what's your good news? I'm dying to hear.'

Simon smiled, obviously still delighted with his news. 'I've been offered a post as junior registrar at the biggest hospital in Leeds. This is just what I wanted! It's a premium post, the department has got an international reputation.'

She threw her arms round his neck, kissed him. 'Simon, I'm so pleased for you! But you deserve the place. You're a wonderful doctor already, and I know you'll easily cope with the new work. Just think, one day I'll be able to say that I knew the famous Dr Simon Bradley when he was young and not famous.'

Simon flushed, looked hesitant. 'Yes, perhaps one day.' he said. 'There are other things. I get a better salary, of course. And they've offered me a flat near the hospital, that's really very nice. It looks as if I'm on my way to a better life. But…'

'Come on,' she said, 'you're with a friend now. What's worrying you?'

'This would have been easier if you hadn't won all that money,' he mumbled. 'Though I was so glad when you did. But there's more to life than money.'

He took a deep breath, seemed to grow stronger. 'I want to ask you if you'd like to come and live with me,' he said. 'Ideally I'd like to marry you. I'd marry you tomorrow, but I know that you've got…well, doubts. But you could live with me and I'd happily wait.'

Petra was shocked and touched. She remembered he had offered her a place before, ultimately it hadn't been necessary. She knew now that he loved her. But… 'Simon, you know I think a lot of you, an awful lot. And I—'

He held up his hand. 'Petra, I know this is something that you didn't expect. And you're still not fully recovered after the Caesarean, you might think you are but you're not. Remember the women you've nursed, who have had disturbances months after they thought they were over everything. So I don't want to push you and I don't want an answer. Think about the offer. And when you're sure—absolutely sure—then let me know.'

She hugged him again, felt a tear run down her cheek. 'You're right,' she said, 'I'm not fully recovered. Look, I'm crying and yet I'm happy. I feel blessed with you as a friend, Simon. So I'll not give you an answer now. But soon I will.'

'That's good enough for me,' he said.

'There's something you can do for me. Eleanor's getting christened next week. Would you like to be her godfather? Let's face it, she owes her life to you.'

He smiled. 'Nothing would please me better,' he said.

He left ten minutes later and she had to sit down. She had thought her life couldn't get more complicated. That's what she had thought. And now this. Could she marry Simon? Her first reaction was a definite no. She would never feel for Simon the passion she had felt for Dominic. Still felt for Dominic. But was passion the only basis for a marriage? Simon was a good, kind, thoughtful man who would love her and Eleanor and any more children they might have. Not that it was that important, but she suspected he would be a successful and popular doctor. But she could never feel for him the— The doorbell rang.

It was Dominic. In his hand he had a bunch of flowers, on his face an expression of irritation. She invited him in. For some reason, whatever they had shared the night before, their very togetherness, seemed to have disappeared.

'I brought you these,' he said, thrusting the flowers at her.

'Thank you, they're lovely.' And they were. Yet more summer roses, in white, red and yellow. Her life recently seemed to be marked with roses. She said, 'Sit down while I go into the kitchen and put them in water.'

'If I may, I'll just go and look at Eleanor.' So he went onto the patio while she found a vase, arranged her flowers.

He came back into the living room when she returned. 'Simon Bradley's just been here,' she said.

'I know. I saw his car outside, I waited until he had gone.'

So Dominic was angry that she had had Simon as a visitor. Well, too bad. 'He's been offered a post in Leeds as junior registrar. He's overjoyed.'

'I'll bet he is. I'm pleased for him.'

'You should be. His efforts saved the life of your daughter.'

Now he had the grace to look shamefaced. 'I've always thought he was an excellent doctor and he deserves to go far. I'd recommend him to anyone.'

'Good. You know I've arranged to have Eleanor christened next week? Well, I've asked Simon to be a godfather. Jack is going to be the other godfather and Jane, Chris Fielding's wife, is going to be godmother.'

'I see. You seem to have everything well in hand. All carefully organised. Even my family.' His voice was cold.

'They are Eleanor's family too now. And they want Eleanor to be part of them. And as to being carefully organised—well, when you're a single mother, then you have to learn to rely on yourself.'

His voice was angry. 'If you had told me earlier I would have…' Then he shrugged. 'There's little point in going over what's already done. I take it I am invited to the christening?'

'Of course. After all, you are the father. It's to be held at St Paul's church and then afterwards a reception at your brother's house. He and Mary were most insistent that we go there.'

'My brother is as good at organising as you are. It

comes of being a solicitor, he likes to be involved. He'll certainly want to be involved with Eleanor. He loves children. But…is Simon a good choice? After all, he'll be away most of the time.'

'Simon is an excellent choice.'

Petra didn't quite know why she did it. Perhaps it was the contrast between the passion she had experienced the night before and the coldness he was showing now. She said something that she knew would provoke him. 'Simon asked me to marry him. He's very willing to commit himself.'

'I see,' said Dominic, and there was ice in his voice. 'And what was your answer?'

'He told me to take my time, to think about it. And I will, but I think I will say no. It wouldn't be fair to him to say anything else.'

'Well, think about it carefully. It might be a good idea to marry him. He's a good man and he's got a good future ahead of him.'

Dominic stood. 'I'd better go. I stole an hour away from work, I'm needed back there. I'll be in touch.' And, without even a kiss on the cheek, he was gone.

She had handled that really well, hadn't she? Petra thought.

When Eleanor had been discharged, Chris Fielding had said that he wanted to see her at least once a week for the next few weeks. Ordinarily Petra would have taken Eleanor to see him at one of his outpatient clinics. But Chris was a friend and Petra was a SCBU nurse so she went to see him in the unit.

First there was the weighing and the quick examination. Petra knew what the results would be. Eleanor was doing fine. So he took her back to his room and they had a coffee each while Eleanor gurgled and wriggled in her carrycot.

'Settling in in your new home?' Chris asked. 'Everything all right there?'

'It's lovely. And Eleanor and I are very comfortable there. Of course, there are problems but we seem to be coping very well. And there are always friends to call on.'

'Quite. So why are you so down? You're trying to hide it but I know you, something's upsetting you. Just baby blues? Or something more?'

She knew she could trust Chris. And she had worked with him, had seen his skill and wisdom in dealing with the problems and occasional tragedies that SCBU seemed to attract. 'It's Dominic,' she said. 'I don't know what to do about him. Or, to be exact, I don't know what to do about myself. And it's making me ill.'

'I see. I take it he's been round to visit you, then? I thought that after your windfall you'd decided to cut him out of your life.'

'I have seen quite a bit of him. He calls because…because he wants to see the baby. He's fallen in love with her.'

'But apparently not with you?'

'Well, if he has, he hasn't said so. Sometimes we get on really well. Other times we either fight or are cold to each other.'

'Do you love him?'

This was the crucial question. And she didn't know

if she could give Chris a straight answer. She didn't really know herself. She thought she loved him, but...
'I haven't been very lucky in falling in love,' she said, 'I don't seem to be very good at it. And, whatever I do, whatever I feel, I've got to put Eleanor first. But...I think I could love him if he'd let me. Sometimes we get on so well but then he hides behind this barrier. And I'm not prepared to put up with it, I've got my own life to lead.'

'I see. Would you like me to have a word with him?'

'No! This is something he sorts out himself, or he sorts it out with me.'

'A good answer,' Chris murmured. 'You say he's making you ill? Because you don't know where you are, what's going to happen, what your future is?'

'That's it exactly.'

'And you don't want this situation to continue. So are you going to give it a time limit? Within a month...two months...three months...either he comes to some sort of agreement with you or you cut him out of your life for ever?'

When Chris said it, it seems so stark, so brutal. But she reluctantly realised that he was right. She had been a victim with Ken, hanging on, hoping that things might improve. And all that had happened had been that they had got worse. She was not going to be a victim again.

'Right,' she said. 'I'll give it time. Some time. But if things don't go right, then I get out of the situation. Like you said, cut him out of my life for ever.'

'If you think that's the right thing to do. Are you going to tell him about this time limit?'

'No,' she said. 'He has to make up his mind without pressure.'

Petra only heard from Dominic once in the next week. And that message was half satisfactory, half unsatisfactory. He phoned her in the afternoon. And the minute the phone rang there was a ring at her door and a loud knock. But she answered the phone first. And her heart gave its customary thump when she heard him for the first time. He sounded friendly, conciliatory.

'Sorry I've not been in touch,' he said, 'and sorry if I was a bit…bit short with you last time I called. Especially after the night before. But work's getting me down. You know they've closed the A and E section in Denham? For a week or two, just until the building work is finished? Well, they're directing all the emergencies here. But none of the staff to cope with them. Sometimes it seems as if we've got ambulances backed up down the drive, it's a madhouse here.'

It was an explanation and a sort of apology.

There was another knock on the door.

'That's OK,' she said. 'I've seen all the builders wandering about the hospital. But you will be able to get to the christening?'

'Of course. Will you dress her in the robe I bought in Amsterdam?'

'I certainly will. We've tried it on, and she looks lovely in it. I hope that—'

This time the knock on the door was less assertive. It suggested that the person knocking had had enough and was about to go. And she knew who it was. Her hot-water boiler had been acting up, and only by ringing round desperately had she been able to get a plumber willing to come out at once. And now it sounded as if he was about to go. So she shouted down the phone, 'Look, I have to go, Dominic, there's someone at the door. Can you ring me back? If you have time?'

'I'll try.'

She didn't have time to analyse his voice, she was running to the front door. She just had to have hot water.

Sunday, the day of the christening.

Petra wondered what the day would bring. This would be the first time that she, Eleanor and Dominic had been seen together in public. He would be seen with his child and...and his child's mother. She wondered how he would take it, what he would say to friends and family. It would have to be embarrassing for him. But, then, she had never known him avoid any kind of confrontation. He wasn't built that way.

She was looking forward to the day. She had been wondering—and hoping. Perhaps things would be settled in some way.

Petra drove cautiously round to Jack's house. She had offered to come early to help prepare things, but Jack had refused. 'This is your day, yours and Eleanor's. You are the guests.' Then he had grinned and said, 'And you'll get your chance to work some other time.'

Petra liked being a member of the family.

She had bought herself a new summery dress in white and silver, and had then gone mad and bought herself a crimson straw hat. Well, why not? Your daughter didn't get christened every day. And Eleanor looked lovely in the robe that Dominic had bought her.

But when she arrived things weren't so good. Jack came out to meet her, looking angrier than she had ever seen him. 'Mary's just had a message from the hospital. Dominic can't come, he's too busy. This is his daughter's christening! He didn't even have the courtesy to phone himself, got some assistant to send a message. I've a good mind to get on the phone and shout until he gets himself here.'

'No,' said Petra, 'I know he is busy. He'll be disappointed, he really wanted to come.'

And so Jack calmed down. And Petra couldn't show how disappointed she was herself.

They went to church and Petra was amazed at the friends who had turned up. She hadn't realised how popular she was. It was a lovely service, with a genial vicar who told them that the more noise babies made, the better he liked it. This was their service.

After the service she walked in the churchyard with Penny. Family and friends stood around in little groups, talking among themselves. And then Penny had to run off to speak to her father and for a moment Petra was on her own.

A pleasant, motherly looking lady approached her.

Petra didn't recognise her, she'd seen her come into the church after the service had started and sit at the back. Perhaps she was a friend of one of her friends.

'Do you think I could I see the baby, please?' asked the lady.

Proudly, Petra folded back the lap of the robe and the lady peered inside. 'She's lovely,' she said. 'She's got her father's lips, hasn't she?'

Petra looked, a little uncertainly. 'You know her father?'

'Dominic Tate. I've known him since he was fifteen. I'm Susie Cash, by the way. I work with Dominic in A and E.'

'You're the ward manager! I recognise your voice now. The nice lady who sent me the flowers—and who bought the chocolates.'

'That's me. It's just that Dominic needs pushing sometimes.'

Susie took out a small silver package, offered it tentatively to Petra. 'I hope you don't mind, but I've bought Eleanor a little gift. It's a locket, she might like it when she gets a bit older.'

Petra took the package. 'Susie, that's lovely of you. Look, we're going back to Jack's house. Won't you come? They'd love to see you.'

Susie smiled. 'And I'd love to but come I'm far, far too tired. I've just finished a fourteen-hour shift. I'd be still there but Dominic sent me home. He'll be mad when he hears I came here instead of going to bed. But that's Dominic. He gets mad but you don't always have to pay any attention to him.'

'No, perhaps you don't,' Petra said. She was realising that Susie was telling the truth about being tired. The smiling face had deep lines of fatigue. 'Is Dominic all right?'

'Apparently he thinks sleep is for wimps. You know there's a big agricultural show on near Calthorpe? It's an annual event, and we always get a rush on in A and E. And just when we're under-staffed. But Dominic thinks he can hold the fort. Single-handed.'

Susie looked at Eleanor again. Then she said, 'I've learned never to interfere with Dominic's life. But I'm very fond of him and I want him to be happy. There's a lot of good in him, Petra. More than he realises himself.'

'Sometimes he has a strange way of showing it.'

'I know that, but it's there. Must go now, Petra. I hope to see you and Eleanor again.' She walked rap-idly away and Petra looked after her. She had only met her for five minutes but she had liked Susie. And she had been impressed by what Susie had said about Dominic. *There's a lot of good in him. More than he realises himself.*

'Come on, Auntie Petra, we're going home now. We're having photographs taken and you said I looked nice in my long dress and that I could have a picture taken holding Eleanor.' This had been the most exciting day in Penny's life for quite some time.

'OK, darling. And I think I'm ready for something to eat.' They walked back to Jack's car.

First there was lavish buffet. There were all sorts of people wanting to congratulate her, to look at the baby. There were quite a few more presents for

Eleanor. Petra enjoyed herself no end. But always there was the slight sadness. It would have been better if Dominic had been by her side. Would he ever be by her side? She didn't know.

There were a lot of photographs taken in Jack's back garden. One was of Sally, Petra and Eleanor—three generations. If it came out well Petra was going to have a copy for her living room. And finally there were a couple of speeches. The baby's good health had to be toasted in champagne.

She had asked Jack if he would like to propose the toast, and he had suggested that Simon do it instead. 'I'd rather be a bit in the background, Petra. And Simon was there for Eleanor when she was first born. He deserves to make the toast.' So she asked Simon and he said he'd be delighted. She could tell that he meant it.

'Ladies and gentlemen, if your glasses are filled, could I have your attention a minute?'

It was a good confident speech. Simon reminded them that Eleanor had been born prematurely, that her life had been in danger. And her life had been saved by the SCBU team.

'I was a member of that team. We work hard for all our babies—but this fight was more important than most because Petra was one of our own. She was a member of SCBU.'

Simon paused, and there was a scatter of applause. He went on, 'Petra was an orphan. But we now see her in the middle of her new-found family. A grandmother, an aunt, an uncle, and, perhaps most important of all, a cousin Penny—all for Eleanor. In time

I can see Eleanor and Penny being a formidable team. Eleanor is doubly blessed in her family.' Again, a scattering of applause.

'But one person isn't here. Dominic, Eleanor's father.'

Petra felt the shiver of apprehension that ran through the group. So far things had gone brilliantly well. Was Simon going to cause trouble? And Petra herself felt suddenly sick. Simon was going to spoil things for her! How could he?

'Dominic wanted to be here, desperately wanted to, but he's in charge of an A and E department at Calthorpe that is understaffed. And we've just heard that there's been a crisis there, every doctor, nurse and technician is urgently needed. So we're sad that Dominic can't be with us. But there is some consolation in knowing that there's a handful of injured people in A and E who are tremendously glad that Dominic is there instead of here. Dominic is saving lives. And I feel sure that when she is old enough to understand such things, Eleanor will be pleased to know that her father chose to be there instead of here.

'Ladies and gentlemen, I give you the toast, Eleanor Sally Morgan.'

The group repeated the toast, clinked glasses. Then the applause was deafening.

After that it was an even greater party. Petra carried Eleanor round so everyone could see her again, then gave her to her grandmother for a while. And she went to look for Simon.

'That was a wonderful speech, Simon,' she said. 'It was kind and generous when you didn't have to be.'

He shrugged. 'Everything I said was true. And if it made you and other people happy, I'm glad.'

'It did, it made them so happy.'

He was looking at her, half apprehensively, half hopefully. She didn't want him to say any more so she quickly said, 'You asked me a question last week, Simon, and told me not to be in a hurry to answer it. Well, I'm still thinking. And I'll answer it soon.'

'You think and I'll hope,' he said. 'And now I'll let you get back to your other friends.'

After that the party started to diminish. Eleanor had to be fed and then, although she was asked to stay, Petra said she thought she'd rather go home and have an early night. It had been an eventful day. Beside, she knew that Mary, Penny and Jack were setting off later to drive south for a holiday. They needed a break too.

Once in bed she thought about Simon. He was a good, kind man. He would work very hard to make her happy, and she knew that with him she would have a good life. Eleanor would have a devoted father.

But it wasn't enough. Own up to it, face it, she was in love with Dominic. And it would be unfair to take Simon, knowing that he was only second best.

So what to do about Dominic? Again she remembered Susie's remark that there was a lot of good in him. Well, it was up to him to show it. She had done as much as she could.

CHAPTER EIGHT

DOMINIC had been scheduled to work the night shift before the day of the christening. With any luck things wouldn't be too busy and he'd be able to grab a few hours' sleep in a bed in the doctors' room. But he wasn't lucky. Nothing really big—but a succession of little cases trickled in at irregular times. Three times he managed to lie down and close his eyes. And three times his shoulder was shaken by Susie. He was needed. In the end he gave up and decided to stay awake.

He wasn't really sure that he wanted to go to the christening. He knew that no one was likely to say anything unpleasant to him. His mother, his brother, his friends wouldn't ask him what he was going to do about Eleanor and Petra. But the unspoken question would be in everyone's eyes. And there would be an accusation too. He had let his child down.

Petra had told him that the child's name was to be Eleanor Sally Morgan. Sally to honour Dominic's mother. She and Petra were getting very close. But what would the group there feel when the surname was Morgan, not Tate? He didn't like to think.

Still, he had said he would be there. And he wouldn't let anyone down.

There was an hour to go before handover and he was really looking forward to a few hours' sleep before he left for the christening. Perhaps he'd feel better then, more certain about what he ought to do and feel. But he needed the sleep!

He was just finishing the notes on his last patient, a farmer who had been making an early start and had tripped and fallen over in his yard. He'd put out a hand to save himself, fallen stiff-armed onto the concrete and fractured the lower end of the radius, near to the wrist. A Colles' fracture, it was called.

'I can't work with my wrist in plaster like this,' he had complained sadly to Dominic. 'This is summer, the busiest time of the year for me. I need to use this arm!'

Dominic had sympathised, but there had been nothing he could do. 'You can't use it,' he had said. 'And if you try to use it, then things will get an awful lot worse. Mr Giddens, I'm sorry, but that's it.'

'Well, thanks anyway, Doctor.'

We all have problems, Dominic had thought.

So, an hour to go. Then Susie put her head round the door and said, 'You're needed. Urgently.'

He looked at her set face and cringed. This was something serious. 'I'm off soon. I'll make a start then Julie Marsden can take over.' Julie Marsden was the other senior registrar. The consultant was away on holiday.

'Julie won't take over. Julie is the patient.'

'What?'

She was a friend and he wanted to help her, but he needed a sleep and he had a christening to attend. He looked down at the pain-racked face below him and tried to look comforting.

'I can diagnose myself if you like,' Julie groaned.
'I've had a bit of a history of a grumbling appendix.
It's always cleared itself up. But I felt sick late last
night. I've been vomiting all night and then the pains
started. Classic. Generalised abdominal pain now
moving to the right iliac fossa.'

'Well, let's see what I can feel,' Dominic said
gloomily.

The nurses had already undressed Julie. Dominic's
touch was as gentle as it could be, but still there was
that harsh intake of breath when he touched the af-
fected area.

'OK, appendicitis,' he said. 'It'll have to come out,
we don't want it bursting. I'll phone through upstairs
to Surgical and they can get you a theatre and so on.'

'Thanks, Dominic. And I'm sorry to leave you
short.'

'Don't worry. I'll get in touch with Denham and
ask them to find me a replacement.'

But as he spoke, he knew it wouldn't be easy.
There had to be a senior A and E doctor on duty. It
would have to be him. And there was that agricultural
fair here at Calthorpe. They'd be busy. This wasn't
turning into one of his better days.

He phoned Denham. They promised, rather hope-
lessly, to do what they could. But could he hang on
for a while? Of course he could. He had to, there was
no choice.

The day got worse. It was hot, more people than
had been expected drove down to the fair, and once
there what seemed like a ludicrous proportion of them
had accidents. Nothing was too serious, it was just

the sheer number of them. 'Have you seen the waiting room?' Susie asked. 'It's like a commuter railway station when there's been a lightning rail strike.'

'Don't tell me,' he said.

Susie volunteered to stay behind as an extra hand and he was glad of her help. But she was older than him, hadn't his resilience. When he saw her drop a tray, and then stagger before bending to pick up the contents, he realised that she had had enough.

'You've been great, Susie,' he said, 'but that's the end. You can't take any more. I'm not asking you, I'm ordering you. Go home.'

'But—'

'Home!' And she went.

And the work kept on coming in, so much so that he had to send word by a junior that he couldn't get to the christening.

'Dr Tate. An ambulance coming in.' One of the more experienced nurses came to call to him. 'Apparent heart attack at the fair. Man apparently enjoying himself, walking round the fair with his family. Aged about seventy, history of heart trouble, paramedics have tried to resuscitate but have not been successful.'

'Let's see what we can do,' Dominic said. But from those few words he knew that there wasn't much hope. He knew the paramedics, they were good.

He waited with the crash team at the front of the department. In the distance they could hear the whining of the ambulance siren and very soon it was there, backing into the slot, the doors already opening.

An old man, strapped into the trolley. Dominic took

one look at the face, then glanced at the paramedic. The paramedic shook his head, stooped to speak quietly to Dominic.

'It was easily ten minutes before we got to him. A policeman had tried mouth to mouth and cardiac massage, but with no result. There's no pulse, no BP. Nothing on the ECG trace. We tried the defibrillator but we didn't expect anything and we didn't get anything.'

'Let's get him into Resuscitation,' said Dominic. 'We can at least try. Do you know his name?'

'His name's Peter Henshaw.' A voice came from the back of the ambulance. 'He's seventy-seven years old and he's had a history of heart trouble. This…this isn't a surprise.'

'Mrs Henshaw,' said the paramedic. 'The patient's wife.'

'I'll get a nurse to look after you, Mrs Henshaw,' Dominic said.

They took Mr Henshaw to the resuscitation room, but everyone there knew that it was a waste of time. There were things to be tried, of course—but it seemed an insult to the dead to carry on pretending that there was something that might possibly work. After a while Dominic said, 'That's it. Does anyone think there's any point in carrying on?'

No one did. And there was other work to do.

Dominic sighed. There were other things that required his attention too. But Mrs Henshaw had to be told. And whatever aid and sympathy the hospital could offer must be hers at once.

Mrs Henshaw was sitting in his room, a nurse by

her side. On the table in front of her was a mug of tea. It was untouched. She looked up as soon as Dominic entered, and he knew that much of what he had to say would be unnecessary. 'He's gone, hasn't he?' she asked. 'In fact, he's been dead since he fell down at the fairground.'

Dominic was silent for a moment. Then he said, 'We did everything that could be done. But it was far too late. Yes, I'm afraid your husband is dead.'

'I thought so. I've been expecting it. In fact, he expected it. We even talked about it.'

'Is there anyone we can get in touch with, Mrs Henshaw? Any family close by?'

'My son, my daughter-in-law and their children. They were with us. I didn't want to frighten the children so I said I'd come in the ambulance on my own. But I think my son will be here soon.'

Dominic turned to the nurse, lifted his eyebrows. She knew what he wanted, went promptly to Reception to leave a message.

'Is there anything at all we can do to help you, Mrs Henshaw? I'd like you to try to drink something. It might... I think you need it.'

'I'll have some tea later. But you can do something for me. I want to see him.'

'It might be an idea to wait a while. We'd like to—'

'I've been married to him for forty-five years! Do you think I care what he looks like?' It was the first time she had raised her voice.

He waited a moment and then said, 'Come with me then.'

They stood side by side looking down at the elderly man. After a moment Mrs Henshaw took the cold hand, held it against her breast. 'We've had our troubles, of course,' she said. 'Everyone does. But for all that time he was a good husband to me. He did what he could for me, he thought of me first. So I'll remember the happiness I've had and that will be enough.'

She looked up at Dominic and he was surprised to see that she was smiling a little. 'You have to take the good times while you can, don't you, Doctor?'

The door opened, the nurse looked in. 'Mr Henshaw's arrived,' she said. 'Would you like me to take over for a while, Doctor?'

'If you would, Lucy.' There was other work for him to do.

Early that evening, just when Dominic was wondering how much longer he could carry on, not one but two doctors walked in. He knew and trusted them both.

'The CEO's sent us, Dominic,' one said. 'We're taking over. We took some finding but he found us. And you're our first case. You're off duty for the next twenty-four hours.'

Dominic found he was swaying as he surveyed them. 'I'll show you where we're up to,' he said.

Somehow he walked to his flat, kicked off his shoes and collapsed straight onto his bed. And instantly he was asleep.

He woke four hours later. He was stiff, his eyes felt as if they were stuck together, his clothes were

sticky on him. But the bone-numbing fatigue had
gone. He still needed much more sleep but he could
think more clearly. He had to think about Petra.
Through no fault of his own he had missed the christening. He wanted to explain why to her.

He dragged himself off his bed, went and showered, shaved, cleaned his teeth. He felt a little better.
He made himself a strong coffee, drank it as he
dressed. Then he thought again.

It was dark outside but it wasn't too late, just gone
half past ten. He could be at Petra's flat in half an
hour. She might not have gone to bed yet. Even if
she was in bed she might not mind too much if he
woke her, explained that he'd had a hard day but that
he needed to see her. Just had to see her. She would
understand. When he told her that he...

That he what? That he loved her? That with time
he could turn into a real husband and father? He
thought of Mrs Henshaw again, he couldn't forget the
old lady's dignity. *Take the good times while you can.*
Time. How important time was. She had had forty-
five years. Perhaps it was time he started a love affair
that would last that kind of time.

He thought of phoning Petra, decided against it.
What he had to say had to be said in person. And he
was still not sure what it was. He just wanted her to
know that he couldn't imagine a future without her
and Eleanor. But especially her. He'd tell her he loved
them both—both together and separately. Did that
make sense? He hoped so.

It was fully dark as he set off and even though he
was desperately eager to see her, he still drove care-

fully. He knew that a few drivers would be drunk. It was up to other drivers to take care. And the road between Calthorpe and Denham was both fast and dangerous.

He saw the accident happen.

There was a long sweeping curve in the road as it ran down into a valley and then up the other side. At the bottom of the valley the curve got tighter, the road curved to cross a bridge. There were signs warning drivers to slow down but they were too often disregarded. This was an accident black spot.

He saw the lights of the car as it accelerated down the road, coming towards him. He watched, horrified, as the driver didn't slow down. He couldn't take the bend at that speed!

Too late, the driver saw the bend ahead. Dominic saw the lights quiver, as if the car had shaken. And then the car was off the road, and he saw the lights cartwheel down towards the stream bed below the bridge.

Dominic cursed. He drove his own car to where the oncoming vehicle had left the road. He pulled well onto the verge, turned on his hazard lights. He took out his mobile and phoned 999. Police and ambulance. Only then did he go to the back of his own car, drag out the emergency bag he always carried in the boot and make his way to the wreck below.

He had a torch, of course, a necessary part of his emergency kit. With it in his hand he cautiously scrambled down towards the wreck.

The car had come to rest on its roof. The lights were still on, illuminating a patch of grass yards away. Dominic remembered advice given to him years before by an old and experienced member of the fire brigade. 'Never rush towards an accident. Give yourself a couple of minutes to look round, work out what could happen. What's certain to happen. And then take things very carefully indeed.'

So Dominic put his bag down and looked round the car. He realised that although it was completely upside down, it was balanced very precariously, high on the bank of the stream. It wouldn't take much to rock it and make it roll even further down, taking any would-be rescuer with it.

He knew he should wait for the experts to come. He didn't intend to. The first hour after an accident was the golden hour, when there was the greatest chance of saving lives.

The car moved when he touched it. Carefully, he managed to kick out the glass from an already smashed window and shone his torch to see what was inside. And when he shone his torch, someone started to scream. Well, that could be a good sign. They were alive. And it was a good, full-lunged scream.

A girl was in the passenger seat, hanging upside down from her safety belt. 'OK,' said Dominic, in as reassuring voice as he could manage. 'Help is here, I'm a doctor. I know it's hard but I want you to try to relax. What's your name?'

The girl stopped screaming. 'Veronica,' she said. Then she started screaming again.

Dominic directed his torch at all parts of her body, he could see no sign of injury. He reached down for her neck, intending to check it. But he could see by

the way that Veronica was shaking her head that there
was little chance of there being serious injury there.
Still. He reached back for his bag, took out a hard
collar and with some difficulty fixed it on her, upside
down.

'Now I'm going to lean in and take your weight,'
he said. 'Then I'll unfasten your safety belt. I want
you to relax, fall on me and I'll hold you and ease
you out.'

It was very awkward working there, bent double,
leaning through the window and with the constant
fear that the car would start to roll. But he managed.
And then he half carried, half dragged the girl a little
way from the car. 'Just lie there,' he said, 'don't move
don't roll over, just lie there. Help's coming. And I'm
going back to see what I can do for your mate.'

The girl carried on screaming, although he suspected there was little seriously wrong.

He went back to the car, shone his torch at the
driver of the car. This was going to be a bigger problem. It looked as if the driver had not been wearing
his safety belt. He was curled up in an ungainly ball
on the roof of the car. Dominic glanced at the now
shattered windscreen. A lot of blood. The lad must
have hit his head, probably crushed his chest against
the now deformed steering-wheel. It was an older car,
there were no air bags fitted.

ABC. Airway, breathing, circulation. Cautiously
Dominic crawled through the window, bent over the
body. As he did so the car rocked. Better be careful.
And there was the smell of petrol. Dominic knew that

modern cars seldom burned with the ease that was
seen in films. However, they did sometimes.

The airway seemed to be clear. The youth was
breathing—just. Circulation, Dominic felt for a pulse
in the neck. Fluttery, fast. As he kept his fingers there
he felt it stop—and then start again. Well, for the
moment he'd just have to hope.

There seemed to be a fair amount of blood about
but as he looked he couldn't see any sign of the puls-
ing that would suggest arterial bleeding. So could he
be moved? Certainly not without a neck brace, and
fortunately Dominic carried two.

As he gently eased the head up to slip the collar
underneath, Dominic felt the car slip a little. He had
to get the lad out. If the car rolled further down the
slope he would be unlikely to survive. Dominic managed to get the collar in place.

He put his hands under the lad's arms, pulled him
backwards, was as gentle as he could be as he man-
oeuvred him out of the window. Beneath them the car
lurched. With one final effort Dominic dragged the
lad clear. Then he smiled. In the distance he could
hear the sound of the ambulance.

Behind him, the car slipped, rolled. As it did so the
door flew open. It smashed into the side of Dominic's
head.

When the paramedics arrived they found three bodies. One was screaming, two were unconscious.

It was always bad news when the phone rang in the
middle of the night. Petra glanced at her bedside

clock—one o'clock in the morning. Who could this be? Already she was expecting some kind of disaster.

It was Sally. Not the calm, confident woman that Petra had come to know, but a terrified parent. 'Petra, you've got to come! I'm sorry to phone you, with the baby and all, but I don't know who else to call. Jack and Mary are away, and… Petra, there's been an accident! Dominic…Dominic, he's really badly hurt!'

Petra's still sleepy brain tried to cope with this. Dominic? Dominic, an accident? How…? Where…? 'Sally, do you know where he's been taken?'

'They didn't take him to his own A and E, they've brought him here to the Wolds Hospital, he's in the neurology department.'

'Neurology? Why? How is he injured?' Petra was beginning to panic herself.

'They said he'd hurt his head.'

Petra shuddered. She'd worked in the neurology department, she'd hated it. 'Where are you now, Sally?'

Sally seemed to be calming down a little, perhaps it was finding someone to confide in. 'I'm at home, I'm just getting dressed. They phoned me, I'm the next of kin. I'm going there at once. Look, I'm sorry I phoned you, there's nothing you can do and with the baby with you, you—'

'I can bring Eleanor with me! She's his daughter. Now don't start worrying yet, keep calm and we'll see what the situation is. I'll be there in half an hour. OK, Sally?'

'There was silence for a moment and then Sally said, 'OK, Petra. And I'm glad that you're coming.'

Perhaps, Petra thought, there was a limit to how much trouble you could comprehend. Dominic was badly injured in the neurology department. She would have thought she'd have had hysterics at the news, been unable to cope. But instead she was calm, She was planning what Eleanor might need, wondering how long they would be at the hospital. It was no good panicking until they knew exactly what the situation was.

Her own calmness frightened her.

She didn't think of what might have happened to Dominic. It was too much to worry about.

Eleanor was transferred quickly to her carrycot, she didn't even wake up. Petra took her normal baby bag with her, it had everything that might be needed in the next twelve or so hours. Then she carried the baby out, got in her car and drove to the hospital. One step at a time. Deal with each crisis as it arose. Don't panic, don't anticipate. You'll know everything in time.

Sally was in her car, waiting for Petra outside the neurology department. She got out and hugged Petra. 'I didn't want to go in on my own,' she said. 'I needed company. I'm glad you're here Petra.' And Petra thought that she was calmer than before.

They went into the neurology department. Petra had worked with Peggy Allen, the senior nurse there on night duty. 'Dr Tate is in Theatre right now,' Peggy told them. 'We got Mr Appleby out of bed. He sent for his team and he's operating at the moment. You've got the best there, there's no one better than Mr Appleby for skull injuries.'

Skull injuries. Petra shuddered. 'We don't know what's happened yet,' she told Peggy. 'All we know is that he's been brought in here. What can you tell us?'

Peggy shrugged. 'I don't know much myself. I gather he'd stopped to help at a road accident somewhere between here and Calthorpe. Got out of his car and now he's a casualty too. Thank heaven the paramedics had the sense to bring him here instead of to A and E at Calthorpe.'

'He's been working for the past twenty hours,' Petra said. 'What was he doing driving here at that time?'

'No idea,' said Peggy.

Petra wondered. Why had he been driving to Denham when he must have been exhausted? Could he have being coming to see her? The idea was ridiculous! Or was it?

Peggy hadn't too much time to talk. She showed them into a waiting room, fetched them tea and her own biscuits and said that as soon as there was any news they'd be told at once. Then they were left alone. Both were nurses. They knew what to expect. No one would tell them anything until the consultant had finished his work.

Eleanor was in her carrycot, on a chair between the two. Every ten minutes Sally would move the little sheet that shaded Eleanor's face and stare at her grandchild. It seemed to bring her comfort.

'At the christening today someone said that she had her father's mouth,' Petra said. 'Can you see a likeness?'

Sally stared even more fiercely than ever. 'I think there is,' she said. 'I think that would be nice. And Dominic was a good baby too.'

Other than that they didn't talk. Each knew the other was thinking the same thing. There was no point in talking.

It gave them a shock when the door suddenly banged open. There was Mr Appleby, the surgeon. A tall thin man still in green scrubs, his cap on his head and his mask still dangling from his neck. Petra had met him before, he was a kind man.

'Dominic Tate. Mother and wife, eh?'

'Mother and partner,' Sally said quickly.

'Well, sorry you had to be pulled from your beds.' He walked over and looked down at the carrycot. 'Who's the little one?'

'That's Eleanor,' said Petra. 'Dominic's daughter.'

'Hmm. Pretty child. Right, well, I've been told you're both nurses, understand the jargon. That helps. Dominic was hit hard on the skull, apparently by a car door. CT scan showed that there was a depressed fracture, subdural bleeding, a lot of pressure on the brain. Cerebral oedema. We've eased the pressure, put him together as best we can. Done all we can, now it's up to him. He's a good strong man, constitution of an ox. With any luck he should be all right. I'm cautiously hopeful.'

'Why only cautiously hopeful?' asked Petra.

He sighed. 'Brain and mind, two different things. The brain we've fixed, reasonably well. But the mind...we don't yet know what effect that nasty knock will have had on his mind. Have to wait and see.'

He looked at the clock on the wall. 'It's the middle of the night, you know. There's nothing more you can do here. There'll be no progress for hours yet, he certainly won't come to. Why don't you both go home, get some sleep, come back in the morning? That's what I'm going to do.'

It was Sally who asked the question that had slowly forced itself on them both. 'He will regain consciousness, won't he?'

'I hope so,' sighed Mr Appleby. 'But we can't guarantee it.'

Dominic had been moved to a side ward, was being specialled by a nurse whose sole job was to keep him comfortable, keep an eye on the battery of instruments that were monitoring his progress.

Peggy took them to see him. Petra recognised—in fact, had used—most of the machines that were now arrayed behind Dominic's bed. There was the pulse oximeter measuring the level of oxygen, the twelve-lead ECG and the large monitor that indicated blood pressure, respiration and all other vital signs. There was an IV line, an oxygen mask. She knew their functions, they didn't frighten her. But it seemed strange to see them hooked up to Dominic's muscular body instead of to tiny babies.

And Dominic seemed diminished. His head was swathed in a cocoon of bandages, his face not recognisable because of the tube leading into his mouth and the oxygen mask.

Almost automatically her eyes turned to the dials

on the machine, checked to see that all was well. Different readings from a thirty-two week baby, but she recognised that all was as well as could be expected.

'You know, there's going to be no real change for the next few hours,' Peggy said. 'If there is we'll certainly phone you. But there's nothing you can do for him now. So, like Mr Appleby says, why don't you go home, try to get some sleep? You're going to need all your strength when he does wake.'

Petra looked at Sally, who nodded. 'All right,' Petra said. 'We'll be back early tomorrow. Sally, will you come and stay with me in my spare room? I'd like us to be together.'

'I'd like that too,' Sally said.

Surprisingly, Petra managed to sleep. It was as if she knew there was nothing she could do, so she might as well conserve her energies for when they would be needed. But just as consciousness finally left her, there was one last thought. She was worried about Dominic, here and now. No longer was there any concern about their future. She just knew that when he recovered, all would be well. It was a comforting thought.

She was wakened at the usual time by the usual baby wail. Sally was already up and dressed, had waited quietly for Petra to appear. 'I want you to be with me when I phone the ward,' she said.

'Let's do it now.'

But there was little news. Dominic appeared to be rallying but hadn't yet regained consciousness. 'It sometimes just happens like this,' the nurse said. 'It's not necessarily bad news.'

Petra and Sally looked at each other but said nothing.

Sally rang Jack, who was obviously deeply upset and said the family would come back at once. Petra and Sally found that bathing and feeding Eleanor then making their own breakfast was some kind of activity that stopped them thinking. Then, with Eleanor in the carrycot as before, they set out for the hospital.

There was a new sister in charge of the ward, but there had been no change in Dominic. Sunlight spilled into the little ward. But Dominic just lay there. Sally and Petra sat by the bed, watched him. After a while Eleanor started to cry. They took it in turns to hold her, to rock her. And then Eleanor gurgled happily.

After about an hour Mr Appleby came to see Dominic. He was now efficient-looking in his white coat, and followed by his retinue of junior doctors and students. Petra and Sally had to leave while Dominic was examined. After the examination Mr Appleby came alone to speak to them, in the waiting room.

'Why hasn't he regained consciousness yet?' Petra asked. 'And how long will it be before he does regain consciousness?'

The consultant glanced from worried face to worried face, and then sighed. 'The honest answer to both questions,' he said, 'is that I don't know.

'The operation was a complete success, we did what was necessary and I'm pleased with his progress. But now he's in a coma. I've tried him on the

Glasgow coma scale, he's only scored three. He may come out of it very soon and there could be no ill effects. I certainly hope so.'

'But the longer he stays in the coma,' said Sally, 'the more unlikely it is that he'll ever come out?'

'True,' Mr Appleby said heavily. 'But let's not think about that yet. I'm glad you're here, his family, the people who know him best. The best thing you can do is talk to him. There's nothing wrong with his hearing, it might be that some message gets through. And if there's any change I'll be here within ten minutes.'

So they sat by Dominic's bed and talked to him. They took it in turns, and talked about anything. Sally talked about his childhood, recollecting episodes that might have stuck in his memory. Petra listened, fascinated, to some of them. So Dominic had been the star boy treble in the local church choir. Chief choirboy? Had sung a solo in York Minster? Who would have thought it?

She herself had less material to work with. She could hardly let his mother hear her talk about their first meeting—well, not all the details anyway. She could mention the fireworks seen through the window. She couldn't mention the incredible sex. Still, she noted that Sally shot her an alert look with a little smile, and so she blushed.

After a couple of hours Sally disappeared for a while, she had to phone the Sandpit crèche to make arrangements there. And when she returned she seemed much calmer, more in control. 'This might be a long haul,' she said. 'It's silly both of us being here.

Why don't you go for a walk—take Eleanor down to SCBU and call on your old friends? They'll be pleased to see you. And right now you need to know that you've got friends.'

Petra thought a moment, looked at Dominic. 'All right,' she said. 'I'll be half an hour.'

Her friends in SCBU had heard about Dominic's accident—no keeping secrets in a hospital. She was taken into the nurses' room, given sympathy and even more coffee and Eleanor was duly admired. 'Definitely one of our successes,' a nurse said.

There were always calls on the nurses' time, and after fifteen minutes Petra was left alone. And then Simon came in. He said as earnestly as he could that he hoped Dominic would recover. Petra hugged and kissed him. Then she said, 'Simon, I'd better tell you now. I'll always be—'

'There's no need,' he said, smiling sadly. 'I can tell Dominic is the one for you. But we'll still be friends. And I am godfather to Eleanor.'

'I think she's very lucky to have you,' Petra said.

She went back to Dominic's little ward, hoping perhaps that there might have been some small change in her absence. But all was as before. His condition was unchanged. 'Now it's your turn,' she said to Sally. 'I've got your mobile number, I can always get in touch. But you go for a walk, call at the Sandpit or something. We're both going to need to keep our strength up.'

So Sally went. But Petra was lonely on her own. She hadn't realised how comforting Sally's presence had been. So she fed Eleanor and rocked her. And as she did she talked to both her daughter and her…her what? What was Dominic to her? One thing she now knew, he was the man she loved. And when he recovered she'd make sure he knew it. How could he frighten her this way?

Sometimes she thought Dominic was regaining consciousness. There would be a blip in the readings, he might stir a little, his eyelids flutter. But then the readings would return to what they'd been before, he'd relapse to stillness again. It was disappointing.

And all the time she talked to him. Now Sally wasn't here she could say anything. So in great detail she told him about their love-making, about how it made her sure that they belonged together, about what they would do when they were together again.

But it didn't work. And after a while the tears came to her eyes. Would it ever work? Would he ever talk to her again…hold her…hold his daughter?

His daughter! Petra had an idea. He hadn't responded to words from his mother or her lover. What about his daughter?

Eleanor was asleep. Gently, Petra picked her up and took off her nightdress. Then she pulled down the sheet that covered Dominic's body and laid her baby between the crook of his arm and his chest. Their skins were touching. There was that indefinable baby smell. And Eleanor seemed comfortable though Dominic didn't move.

Petra remember that afternoon on the beach when Dominic had dozed a little with Eleanor on his bare chest. The two had looked so good together there.

Was there some kind of a memory locked in his mind?

She whispered to him. 'That's your baby, Dominic. Your baby Eleanor. She wants her daddy, wants him to wake and hold her. Can't you feel your baby, Dominic?'

It didn't seem to work. Dominic remained still.

After a while Eleanor woke. Petra saw her wriggle a little, the tiny arms stretch out as if in protest. Then there was the first cry, weak at first, but Petra knew that they would get stronger. Eleanor was developing a fine pair of lungs.

Another cry, this time stronger. Perhaps Petra should pick up her baby, nurse her. But, no, she'd leave her there a while longer. A much stronger cry. Petra remember the old wives' tale that a mother could hear her baby cry in the middle of the loudest storm. Did it work for fathers? No storm, but Eleanor gave the loudest cry yet, and indicated that she was not going to stop.

Petra sighed, leaned forward and reached for Eleanor. And as she did so she looked at Dominic's face. Did his eyelids twitch? She let Eleanor cry a bit more. Yes, Dominic was trying to open his eyes! It was working!

She leaned back, almost automatically checked the monitors behind him. There seemed to be activity in some of them. Dominic was coming round!

The nurse entered the room, feet pattering. She glanced at the monitors, leaned over to examine Dominic. 'Fantastic! This is more than a blip, I think he's coming round. I'm going to bleep Mr Appleby, he'll be so pleased.' Then she looked at Eleanor, grinned at Petra. 'A new discovery. I've never seen a baby used as a resuscitation aid before.'

'It worked,' Petra said, through her tears.

Now she reached and took Eleanor but her eyes were focused on Dominic. Now she could see his chest rising and falling, his breathing was deepening to cope with the increased blood pressure, the more rapidly beating heart. His hands clenched and relaxed, there was the beginning of a moan. Dominic was coming to!

His head turned. His eyes opened, blinked but then stayed open but unfocused. The nurse handed Petra a dampened tissue, she leaned close and wiped his face. The little stimulus seemed to work.

Petra saw his eyes clouded with doubt. Then, slowly, sense seemed to appear in them. He focused, he knew who he was, perhaps even where he was. His lips seemed to move, Petra wiped them for him. Three times he tried. Then he spoke. 'Good to see you, sweetheart,' he said.

After that things seemed to happen at an ever increasing speed. Mr Appleby appeared, still followed by his cohorts of juniors. Petra and Eleanor were shooed out of the room. Dominic had to be examined. Then his dressing had to be reapplied. He had to be washed, made more presentable.

Petra made a cautious phone call to Sally. 'I think it's good news—certainly it isn't bad. He seems to be coming round. He recognised Eleanor.'

'Oh, thank God!' Just one gasp, but it reminded

Petra that Sally would feel for Dominic what she felt for Eleanor. 'I'll be with you in ten minutes.'

'Take it steady. We don't want another crash and the doctors are looking at him.'

And then Mr Appleby came in to see her. He was smiling. 'Things seem to be progressing well now,' he said. 'Of course, he's not out of the woods yet. There could be a relapse—though it's unlikely. There will certainly need to be a period of recuperation. But…I'm very pleased.'

'May I see him now?'

'Of course. And he wants to see you. You know the usual things that doctors say to patients' relatives—don't overtire him, don't expect too much too soon. But go and see him at once. It's therapeutic.'

He opened the door and then turned to say, 'By the way, the nurse told me about using the baby to wake him. That was brilliant.'

'Thank you,' Petra said.

Dominic looked more alert now. He didn't need the oxygen mask or the tube into his mouth. When she entered the room his head turned, his eyes focused. She knew he recognised her and her heart nearly burst with happiness. She kissed him on the cheek.

'You frightened me,' she whispered to him. 'I thought I'd lost you.'

'I wouldn't leave you. Petra, there's things I've got to…we have to…'

She kissed him again. 'Not now,' she said. 'We'll talk later. You know I'm here for you.'

'Talk later,' he murmured, and she saw his eyes

closing. Then his eyes opened again. 'Where's my...? Where's our...daughter?'

Petra took Eleanor from her carrycot, held her so that the tiny sticky lips touched his cheek. 'Eleanor's glad to see her daddy's better,' she said.

This time his eyes closed and didn't reopen.

Petra scanned the monitors again. Not a coma, just sleep. Good.

CHAPTER NINE

AFTER the heart-shaking excitement, it was amazing to discover that ordinary life had to go on.

Sally came in ten minutes later, breathless and desperately hopeful. Dominic opened his eyes just long enough to mutter, 'Hi, Ma, I'm doing fine.' Then he went to sleep again. But it was long enough for Sally. For the first time, she burst into tears.

Shortly afterwards Jack and Mary came into the ward. They had driven up from the south coast and were weary but determined to see Dominic at once.

'Too many visitors,' said Petra, knowing how this could tire a patient. 'Where's Penny?'

Jack said, 'We left her outside, just for a while. We didn't want her to see...to see her uncle like this.' Then he said, 'We didn't know what we'd find ourselves.'

'It was so much worse this morning,' Sally said.

Petra thought that perhaps it was time she left. She wanted to stay, but life did have to go on. 'Why don't I pick up Penny and take her to my flat?' she asked. 'I can tell her about Dominic and she can help me with Eleanor.'

Everyone thought that was a good idea. So Petra went to the car park, collected Penny and went home.

She didn't know how she felt. In fact, she felt nothing. It was as if the high emotion of the last twenty-four hours had been so much for her that she couldn't feel any more. Just giant relief. Dominic was going to be all right.

Calming Penny was another thing entirely. Dominic was her favourite uncle. In fact, he was practically her only uncle as Mary's two brothers lived in Australia. 'Are you sure he's going to be all right?' she demanded. 'Did the doctor say that he was definitely all right?'

'Doctors tend not to say that kind of thing. They need to be absolutely certain. But I'm sure.'

And this seemed to satisfy Penny. But perhaps because she was still worried, or perhaps because her parents weren't there to stop her, Penny felt she was entitled to ask a couple of awkward questions.

'Are you going to marry Uncle Dominic?'

Petra considered how she should answer. And she knew she'd be answering herself as well as Penny. 'I don't know. I haven't known him very long and he hasn't asked me. For the moment all I want is to get him better.'

Penny was not going to be put off with this. 'You knew him long enough so you could have a baby together. Anyway, I thought people were supposed to get married before they had babies.'

'It's usually considered a good idea,' Petra said cautiously, 'but it doesn't always happen.'

'Why didn't Uncle Dominic tell us he was having a baby?'

'Because I didn't tell him,' said Petra.

'He would have wanted to know. Not telling him was a bit mean, wasn't it?'

Petra thought for quite a while. 'I suppose it was,' she said.

'Well, when he gets better, and if he asks you, will you marry him? Do you love him?'

Petra knew that, she should gently tell this child that it was rude to ask personal questions. But she didn't want to. She didn't feel like it. 'Yes, I'd marry him and, yes, I love him,' she said. 'Now, what do you want for tea?'

But Penny was not going to be deflected. Petra saw a lot of Dominic's determination in her. Was it an inherited trait? Was Eleanor going to be as tough-minded as this child?

'Are you going to tell him that you want to marry him and that you love him? 'Cos if you're not, I want to tell him myself.'

'Penny! That's just not the way you go about things. Leave Uncle Dominic and me to sort out our own affairs. Now, what do you want for tea?'

'I heard Mummy and Dad talking in the car when they thought I was asleep,' Penny said sulkily. 'Daddy said that you were the best thing that had ever happened to Uncle Dominic, and if he didn't grab you quick some other lucky man would. And I don't want that to happen.'

'How about a couple of poached eggs on toast?' suggested Petra.

Sally, Jack and Mary called later to pick up Penny and give a progress report. They said that Dominic was improving every hour, that a young doctor had been in and said he was making a wonderful recovery. Then they set divided up the visiting times.

'Would you like to go tomorrow morning?' Jack asked Petra. 'Or would it be better for Eleanor if you went later?'

'I'd like tomorrow morning. And Eleanor is no trouble. I think she likes the ride.'

'Settled, then. Would you like to come back to our house for a late supper?'

'Not tonight, thank you. I'm going to bed early. I need a good night's sleep.'

'I think we all do,' said Sally.

Just before getting into bed, Petra phoned the ward. Peggy's cheerful voice said, 'He's sleeping like a baby, he's the best patient we have.'

'Just wait till he wakes up a bit more. He likes his own way and he doesn't mind telling people about it.'

'Not on my ward,' said Peggy, and Petra went to sleep happy.

Petra couldn't believe the improvement next morning. Dominic was sitting up, she was told he'd just had a light breakfast. He smiled at her when she entered, and the contrast between this morning and yesterday at the same time was enough to make her cry.

She leaned over to kiss him. He managed to get an arm round her and give her a gentle hug. 'Why the tears? That's not much of a greeting.'

'Because I'm happy,' she said. 'Because I'm so happy. Now, how are you?'

'I feel as if I've lost a fight with a steamroller and I've got a headache that no aspirin will ever remove. Otherwise I'm good. Now, may I see my daughter?'

Petra lifted the carrycot for him to see and for a moment he said nothing. 'My mother said that Eleanor brought me back to consciousness,' he said. 'But I think it was you.'

'We both love you,' said Petra. Then she stopped, confused. 'There, I've said it,' she said, 'and I didn't intend to.'

'Well, I like it, I like being loved. And, Petra, there's something I've got to say to you. About you and me and Eleanor. I know I haven't been the most brilliant of suitors, and perhaps you don't—'

She held up her hand stopped him. 'Please, Dominic, don't say any more. Not yet anyway. I've got a suggestion.'

She saw that he looked disappointed, so she hurried on, 'You've had a nasty trauma to the head, your feelings are bound to be all over the place. You're not sure what you're saying. I've had no trauma but I've had a bad couple of days. And now I'm so happy I could scream with joy. My emotions are all too much again. So what I'm suggesting is that we put off talking, say, for a week. That is, talking about us. Seriously talking about us.' Then she looked at him doubtfully. 'You do want to talk about us, don't you?'

'Seriously?' he teased. 'Oh, yes, I do. Very seriously.' He thought for a moment and then said, 'All right, we'll wait exactly a week. Then we'll—'

Her mobile phone rang. She should have turned it off when she had come into the hospital but she had forgotten. She checked the number. Jack's house. So she answered and it was Penny.

'Are you seeing Uncle Dominic now?'

'Yes, Penny, I am.'

'Are you going to tell him that you love him?'

'I already have done.'

'And are you going to—'

'Penny! I thought we had an agreement. Just give us time.'

'Well, I'm looking through this magazine and it's got these pictures of bridesmaids' dresses and I thought that I'd look nice in a pink one.'

'I'm sure you would. I'll look at the magazine with you. But not yet! Now, I'm going to hand you over to Uncle Dominic, and you be careful what you say to him because he'll tell me everything.'

All right,' said Penny, and Petra handed over the mobile to Dominic.

He listened for a while, smiled and said, 'That'll be lovely. Looking forward to seeing you too, Penny. Yes, I love you too.'

He handed to mobile back to Petra, and she could tell he was tiring. 'OK,' he said, 'we wait a week. Then we'll talk. It might be a good thing to wait, head wounds can be funny things. I could have some kind of regression, a character change or whatever. Then you'd have to think again.'

She was upset. 'That's not what I'm worried about! To me, you're you, whether injured or not. I'm not going to change the way I think about you just because of some accident.'

He smiled. 'I could have guessed you'd say that. But accidents do have effects. I still have no idea what happened that night. I've got retrospective amnesia.'

She dismissed that. 'That's nothing. Mr Appleby says it's nothing and we're not to worry about it.'

'OK, then.' He was silent for a while and then said, 'One thing I do want you to know now. When I got hurt I was on my way over to see you. I had things to say to you. Things I still will say to you.'

'I know you were coming to see me,' she said. 'Well, at least I guessed. Now you're tired. Slide down that bed and go to sleep. I'll sit here quietly.'

He stretched his arm out a little. 'Put Eleanor here for a while, will you?' he said. So she did.

Dominic improved greatly over the next week, Petra was convinced that he did it by sheer determination. By then he was washing and shaving himself, talking about what he would do when he was discharged.

He knew he couldn't return to work for some time. The high pressure of life in an A and E unit would be far too much for him, and he had the sense to realise it. He would have to convalesce.

Petra thought that the best place for him to convalesce might be her flat. But she hadn't suggested it yet. Not to him anyway. Sally thought it was a great idea.

And now the week's silence she had asked him for was at an end. They had to talk. He had told her this that night before and she had nodded, accepting it. But she had not slept too well. There was a sense that her life might be about to change.

They were sitting outside now. There were French windows in the ward that opened onto a grassy area outside. It was sunny, he had Eleanor on his lap.

'So the week you asked for has passed,' he said. 'We have a date, we have to have a conversation.'

'If you want,' she said. She felt slightly light-headed.

'I think I'm glad you made me wait,' he said. 'Though I haven't changed my mind a bit. I think now just as I did seven days ago. But at least we both know I'm not concussed or anything like that.'

'I gather Mr Appleby's been to see you.'

'Told me to go home. Said I was cured, that there was nothing wrong with brain or mind, that I was taking up a bed that someone really needed. But he'd let me stay another couple of days.'

'A consultant of the old school.'

'True. So we both know that I know what I'm doing, what I'm saying. And now I realise that I didn't know that before. I mean before the accident.'

'I know what you mean,' she said. 'You don't like accidents, you've always been someone who wants to be in control. You make the decisions about the future. But now you know that sometimes it's not possible. And even good things can come about without you having planned them.'

He bent his head over the child on his lap. 'Your mother's says you're a good thing, little one,' he whispered, 'and she doesn't mind that you weren't planned.'

'I didn't mean her at all!'

Then she saw that he was laughing at her. After a while he said, 'I told you this when I first came to, and I want to tell you again. When I had the accident I was on my way to see you. I wanted...I wanted to

tell you I loved you. That was to be all then. I thought
we'd wait for a while, we'd get to know each other,
we'd get our lives sorted out and then perhaps, in a
few months, or even weeks…well, who knows?'

'I first met you nine months ago,' she pointed out.
'And though we didn't meet for nearly eight of them
afterwards…I did think of you a lot. It's odd. I think
I knew that you might be angry but that you'd want
to help. In fact, insist on helping. Which is why I
didn't get in touch. I wasn't confident with men, I'd
not had too much luck. That night we spent together
was magic. I didn't want it spoiled by dreary argu-
ments over money. I didn't want you to turn into another Ken.'

He winced. 'What a fate.'

She could always tell when he was thinking. He'd
frown a little. And if he had Eleanor on his lap, he'd
stroke her back, a gentle fingertip caress that she obviously loved.

'The big question is why I didn't get in touch with
you,' he said eventually, 'and this week I've thought
about it a lot. That night was magic for me too. And
half a dozen times I picked up the phone to ring
you—then I put it down.'

'You warned me I wasn't to expect anything. That
was good of you.'

'That was me trying to keep my conscience clear.
But you were different. And until recently I thought
the reason I didn't phone you was because I thought
I could sense a hunger in you, a need for love and
commitment.'

'I didn't know I was so obvious,' she said sadly.

'You weren't obvious. Anyway, I got things completely wrong. I thought that I was keeping away from you because I just didn't need that kind of commitment. I preferred my own way of carrying on. And then it came to me. I was just plain scared.'

'Because of Alice. You didn't want to go through that pain again.'

'True. And one of the things that has been hurting me all week is that I've just put you through what I had to suffer. How did you feel when you thought I might die, Petra?'

'I don't want to think about it any more,' she said, dry-lipped.

'No. So there's the two of us making mistakes and assumptions. We could have been so happy over the past nine months. So have we learned?'

'We've learned. And we were getting there before your accident. Things were better.'

'So they were.' He pulled Eleanor a little closer to him. 'But then I had the accident. I've been not too far from death. And I realise now that it's not a good idea to hang about.'

He put his hand in his dressing-gown pocket.

'Jack came to see me yesterday afternoon. I asked him to do a bit of shopping for me. He came back last night.'

Dominic opened his hand, there was a small leather box. He flicked it open, there was a diamond ring, the most beautiful ring she had ever seen.

'We've both made mistakes, but we've been lucky and we've been blessed with Eleanor. Now I want to be doubly blessed. Will you marry me, Petra?'

Over the past few weeks she had shed more tears than ever in her life before. And now, once again, her eyes brimmed. But this time through happiness.' Oh, yes. I'll marry you, Dominic. I love you so much.'

He was holding Eleanor, there wasn't too much she could do. But she stood and kissed him. Then she kissed her baby's head.

'We'll be such a happy family.'

Modern Romance™
...international affairs – seduction and passion guaranteed

Medical Romance™
...pulse-raising romance – heart-racing medical drama

Tender Romance™
...sparkling, emotional, feel-good romance

Sensual Romance™
...teasing, tempting, provocatively playful

Historical Romance™
...rich, vivid and passionate

Blaze Romance™
...scorching hot sexy reads

27 new titles every month.

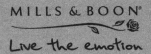

MILLS & BOON®

Live the emotion

Medical Romance™

IN DR DARLING'S CARE by *Marion Lennox*

Dr Lizzie Darling runs into her new boss, the gorgeous
Dr Harry McKay, on her first day at work and breaks his
leg! But she doesn't want to be a family doctor, or to get
involved in the tiny community of Birrini. She doesn't
want to get involved with Harry either, no matter how
attractive he is! But now, as the only available doctor,
she has no choice but to stick around…

A COURAGEOUS DOCTOR by *Alison Roberts*

Dr Hugo Patterson had his life just how he wanted it
– until a flame-haired firebrand called Maggie burst in
and turned it upside down. The sparky paramedic
found Hugo's reserved charm irresistible, and she
was determined to help him loosen up – but there
was no way the dedicated doctor would fall for
someone like her…

THE BABY RESCUE by *Jessica Matthews*

Bk 2 of Hope City

At Hope City Hospital, locum Nikki Lawrence is
taking on more than she bargained for. Not only is
she working with the man who broke her heart, she
also has to rescue a baby abandoned by its mother!
But gorgeous physician Galen Stafford still loves Nikki
beyond anything – can he persuade her that some
bonds remain unbreakable?

On sale 4th June 2004

*Available at most branches of WHSmith, Tesco, Martins, Borders,
Eason, Sainsbury's and all good paperback bookshops.*

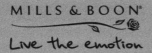

MILLS & BOON®

Live the emotion

Medical Romance™

THE CONSULTANT'S ACCIDENTAL BRIDE
by Carol Marinelli A&E Drama

An accident forces emergency nurse Leah Jacobs to share a home with A&E consultant Cole Richardson. His ice-cool reserve is driving her mad, but the drama and emotion of A&E give her a glimpse of his tender side. And then a major incident brings back memories that Cole has buried deep inside...

THE REGISTRAR'S SECRET *by Judy Campbell*

Dr Emma Fulford was determined to be relationship-free – so she didn't expect to fall for the infuriatingly attractive Dr Sean Casey. But when the two registrars had to work side by side in the hustle and bustle of A&E, there was no way they could ignore the sparks flying between them!

CHALLENGING DR CARLISLE *by Joanna Neil*

Dr Sarah Carlisle is in love with the wrong man – her boss! How can she care for someone who abandoned her sister when pregnant? Working with the devilishly sexy Dr Matthew Bayford is a challenge, but soon Sarah discovers he isn't as off-limits as she thought. Her sister's baby isn't his, for a start...

On sale 4th June 2004

Available at most branches of WHSmith, Tesco, Martins, Borders, Eason, Sainsbury's and all good paperback bookshops.

0504/03b

MILLS & BOON

Summer
Temptations

Lori Foster
Kristine Rolofson

On sale 4th June 2004

Available at most branches of WHSmith, Tesco, Martins, Borders,
Eason, Sainsbury's and all good paperback bookshops.